Private Eyes

Private Eyes

Jasmine Cresswell

THORNDIKE
CHIVERS

This Large Print edition is published by Thorndike Press®, Waterville, Maine USA and by BBC Audiobooks, Ltd, Bath, England.

Published in 2004 in the U.S. by arrangement with Harlequin Books S.A.

Published in 2004 in the U.K. by arrangement with Harlequin Enterprises II, B.V.

U.S. Hardcover 0-7862-6347-4 (Romance)
U.K. Hardcover 0-7540-9878-8 (Chivers Large Print)
U.K. Softcover 0-7540-9879-6 (Camden Large Print)

All characters in this book have no existence outside the imagination of the author and have no relation whatsoever to anyone bearing the same name or names. They are not even distantly inspired by any individual known or unknown to the author, and all incidents are pure invention.

The text of this Large Print edition is unabridged.
Other aspects of the book may vary from the original edition.

Set in 16 pt. Plantin by Christina S. Huff.

Printed in the United States on permanent paper.

British Library Cataloguing-in-Publication Data available

Library of Congress Cataloging-in-Publication Data

Cresswell, Jasmine.
Private eyes / Jasmine Cresswell.
p. cm.
ISBN 0-7862-6347-4 (lg. print : hc : alk. paper)
1. Brothers and sisters — Fiction. 2. Trials (Kidnapping) — Fiction. 3. Large type books. I. Title.
PR6053.R467P75 2003
823′.914—dc22 2003071128

Private Eyes

Chapter One

Franklin Gettys slammed down the phone and swung around, fists clenched and cheeks flushed with anger. For a moment Helen thought he was going to hit her but, at the last second, he regained control of himself and stepped away.

"That phone call was from Charlie Quarrels at the Half Spur ranch," Franklin said. "My foreman tells me you drove out there on Friday and were poking around the place for most of the day."

"Well, yes, I was there," Helen admitted, wondering what she'd done wrong this time. "The spring sunshine was so great, I took a picnic lunch —"

She didn't have the chance to make any more excuses. Franklin stormed across the room and marched her backward until she was pinned against the bedroom wall, with his hands splayed on either side of her head. "Stop trying to elbow your way into every damn corner of my life," he said, his voice cracking with rage. "Don't try to defy me, Helen, because it won't work. You're moving way out of your league when you pick a fight with me."

"But I wasn't trying to pick a fight," Helen protested. She was trembling inside, but for once she didn't retreat into apologetic silence. For a moment she seriously considered doing something outrageous, like kneeing her husband in the groin so that she could break free of his hold, but sanity — or fear — prevailed. "I would never have gone to the ranch if I'd realized it would make you angry," she said apologetically.

"Then why didn't you tell me you'd been out there?" Franklin demanded. "Why all the secrecy if the trip was so innocent?"

Because you never bother to ask about what I've been doing while you're away in Washington, and it didn't occur to me to tell you, Helen thought. She didn't explain that to Franklin, though, because she was afraid it might sound like a complaint. Her husband didn't deal well with complaints.

"You were tired when you came home last night and we didn't talk much about anything," she suggested meekly.

Somewhat appeased, Franklin pushed away from the wall, releasing her. "Well, don't go behind my back again. I'm not just angry. I'm mad as hell."

"But why are you so mad?" Helen asked, finding a remnant of courage and not letting the subject drop as she would have done normally. "What's wrong with me visiting the Half Spur, since we own it? You've been in Washington for ten days, so it didn't interfere with your plans. I was alone here in Denver and it seemed such a long time since I'd been out of the city. . . ."

"*You* don't own the Half Spur ranch," Franklin said cuttingly. "*I* own it. For the last time, keep your nose out of my private business affairs, Helen, and that's an order."

About to whisper an apology and sneak out of the bedroom, Helen suddenly despised herself for being such a coward. Franklin's behavior was totally unreasonable, so why in the world did she feel guilty? "I didn't harass the sheep, or interfere with the men working at the ranch," she said. "I barely spoke to them, in fact. You need to be more specific about what I did that was so terrible."

"You went where you weren't invited," Franklin snapped, slapping his fist into the palm of his other hand in a gesture that struck Helen as deliberately threatening. "Before you set off on your next wild-goose chase onto my property, ask my permission first. Do we understand each other?"

Helen nodded. Her view of marriage was practical rather than romantic, which was how she'd ended up married to Franklin in the first place. But she'd certainly never dreamed that she would one day find herself ordered to ask permission for something as simple as making a day trip out of Denver. How in the world had her marriage degenerated to this point, she wondered. How had she let herself slide into such a humiliating state of inferiority?

For the second time in as many minutes, Helen failed to share her thoughts with her husband. The past two years had taught her that Franklin's view of marriage was light years away from her own. Her husband wanted a relationship where all the power was his, and all the submission hers. Any attempt to carve out a more independent role resulted in outbursts of violent temper that reminded her all too vividly of her father and left her sick to her stomach.

It was true that Franklin gave her a generous monthly allowance and for a while, early in their marriage, her shiny new credit cards had created the illusion of freedom. She'd even congratulated herself on being sensible, and rejecting the lure of passion and romance offered by her relationship with Ryan Benton. But Helen soon realized that parting from Ryan hadn't just meant the loss of romance in her life. It had meant the loss of hope and fun and laughter as well. Franklin's money came with very long strings attached. He had stated many times that since he paid all the bills, he had the right to demand that she should obey him completely. The trade of freedom for financial security might have suited some women. Unfortunately, Helen didn't find shopping much of a substitute for having friends and an interesting job, much less for surrendering the right to a mind and opinions of her own, and for giving up on any chance of real companionship in her marriage.

She was bone weary of her unequal relationship with Franklin, Helen reflected. She was tired of being humiliated, tired of being made to feel inferior. Her stomach lurched as she confronted the fact that she had finally arrived at the end of her emotional rope. That rope had been long and thick, but this morning marked a turning point in her marriage to Franklin. After two years of nonstop retreat from confrontation, her back was pinned against the wall — figuratively as well as literally — and she had no choice but to stand up for herself and fight.

It took every ounce of her available courage, but she drew herself up and turned around so that she could look straight into her husband's eyes. "Franklin, we have to talk some more about this —"

"Not now," he said, sounding impatient. "I'm late, since you neglected to wake me up on time."

She could have reminded him that she'd tried to wake him twice, and he'd told her to get the hell away and leave him to sleep, but it seemed a waste of breath and energy. She knew he would merely twist her excuses around so that she would end up taking the blame not only for letting him oversleep, but for a bunch of other supposed marital sins as well.

"I need help, Franklin," she said, instinctively retreating into the placating tone which was her usual method of conversing with her husband. This time, though, the humility was false. He might not be aware of what was at stake right now, but she knew their future was on the line. She was offering her husband one last chance to suggest how they might get their marriage onto a healthy footing, a foundation that promised both of them at least a shot at happiness. Both of them, instead of just him.

"I'm feeling lost, Franklin, and I need

your guidance," she said. "What am I supposed to do with myself all day? You don't want us to have children —"

He made a brusque chopping gesture and marched toward his walk-in closet. "For God's sake, don't start that pointless discussion again. I don't want kids. I never suggested we would have kids, and I haven't changed my mind. End of story. End of discussion."

"I'm not starting that discussion again," Helen said, aware that Franklin was correct, and this was a subject they'd beaten to death and beyond. She'd mentioned her desire for children on several occasions during their brief engagement and Franklin had simply failed to respond. She'd interpreted his silence as agreement that they would start a family soon after they married. In retrospect, Helen realized how foolish she'd been to make that assumption. On a subject as important as whether or not he wanted children, she should have confronted Franklin head-on, explicitly spelling out her own desire to have at least one child, and preferably two.

Unfortunately, in those early days of their relationship, she'd been so blinded with happiness that a man as important and famous as Franklin Gettys wanted to marry her that she hadn't cared to probe too hard into the roots of her happiness. It wasn't every day that a United States senator and former football hero asked a twenty-six-year-old casino dancer to marry him, and Helen had been floating on a cloud of euphoria from the time of their first date until the moment she said "I do."

She had spent the past two years learning the grim lesson that a handsome, rich husband was no great catch if he despised you. And even less of a catch when you realized you were beginning to despise him right back.

"I can't spend all day every day shopping, so what am I supposed to do with my time?" she asked, emboldened by desperation. "You ordered me to resign when I volunteered at the local homeless shelter. Same thing when I tried to raise funds and start a day-care center for single moms. You won't let me get a job —"

"You're not qualified for any job suitable for a senator's wife," Franklin said, opening a locked drawer in the dresser to select a pair of cufflinks. The drawer was kept locked because Franklin suspected Mercedes, their housekeeper, would rob him blind if given half a chance. Mercedes was an immigrant from Central America, and Franklin had instructed Helen never to trust her around money or valuables, because immigrants didn't share the values of "real" Americans.

Helen realized she was getting angry just watching her husband lock the drawer and return the key to his pocket. Mercedes didn't deserve the insult. In Helen's opinion, their housekeeper's ethical standards were a lot higher than Franklin's. But since she could only fight one battle at a time, she brought her attention back to the subject they were discussing. "I could help with your reelection campaign —"

"Doing what?" Franklin asked, sticking out his chin so that he could fasten the top button on his shirt. "Political campaigns require brains and education. You don't have either."

Helen flinched, but continued doggedly. "I could address envelopes. I could answer the phone. I'm used to dealing with people, and I think I could be friendly and polite, even in difficult situations. A waitress has to learn how to handle guests who are making unreasonable demands —"

"You think the fact that you were once a waitress qualifies you to talk to people calling my office?" Franklin laughed incredulously, then shook his head. "I wouldn't let you near any phone of mine. God knows what you might say to some important donor that would piss him off."

"Nothing rude or inappropriate, I'm sure." Helen was stung into defending herself.

Franklin rolled his eyes. "Right." He finished sliding polished ebony links into his shirt cuffs and began to knot his silk Givenchy tie. "The last time you chose to spout off your mouth at a fund-raiser, you started lecturing one of my biggest donors on the dangers of biochemical weapons. He happens to be one of the country's leading advocates of increased funding for biological warfare programs, and every damn thing you said offended him. I nearly lost him as a contributor to my reelection campaign, thanks to you."

"I didn't lecture," Helen protested hotly, the injustice of the accusation making her burn inside. "Your donor suggested that the best protection against dictators with weapons of mass destruction was to manufacture a huge supply of our own biochemical weapons. And I simply responded that it could be dangerous for us to stockpile such potent weapons. A terrorist would only need to steal a vial of smallpox, or bubonic plague, and we could have a deadly nationwide epidemic in no time flat. Thousands of American citizens could die —"

"I'm sure my campaign donor was aware of the problems before you gave him the benefit of your ill-considered opinions."

She gritted her teeth, ignoring the insult. "I don't believe your donor had given five seconds of thought to the problems of safe storage. He just wanted Congress to authorize a new weapons research program so that he could spend millions of taxpayer dollars on his pet project. He for sure didn't suggest any ways to solve the problems I'd raised."

"Because you were talking garbage and it wasn't worth his time to correct all your mistaken conclusions. You need to keep your opinions on complicated subjects like this to yourself. Take a tip from me, Helen. Don't try to appear smart, and then you won't embarrass both of us by displaying your ignorance."

Her husband certainly knew how to wound her, Helen thought, shriveling into silence. She was always painfully conscious of the fact that she had no college degree. However hard she'd tried to improve her general knowledge over the past couple of years, her constant reading was probably not enough. She was miserably aware that there could be gaps in her basic education that she wasn't even aware of, gaps that validated Franklin's opinion of her stupidity.

Tears burned at the back of her throat and she swallowed hard, banishing them before Franklin could be aware of how his jibes had hit home. Tears and self-pity never got a person anywhere worth going, Helen reminded herself. She'd learned that lesson years ago, when she was fourteen and her mother had died. Her father had just about drowned in grief and bitterness, leaving Helen to take care of the house, the bills and her desolate younger brother. Even at fourteen, she'd thought that her father's wallowing self-pity had been a pretty crummy way to honor her mother's memory.

Helen sighed, making one last effort to show Franklin how his various rules and edicts left her with a life that was empty of worthwhile activities. "If I can't even offer my honest opinion about important political issues, what is there left for me to do?" she asked. She hoped against hope that her husband would take the question seriously and make a constructive suggestion in response. "I want to help you, Franklin. I want to be part of your life. Just tell me how."

"You could start by showing a bit more enthusiasm in the bedroom," he said. "I'm sick to death of sleeping with a woman who doesn't even bother to fake orgasms anymore. Sex with you is about as exciting as taking a plastic doll to bed."

She blushed. "I'm sorry," she said huskily. "I realize I haven't been too much fun as a lover recently. . . ."

"Fun?" He snorted. "There's an understatement if ever I heard one. You don't seem to know what the word means anymore." He shrugged into his blazer and stepped back to look at himself in the mirror. He was scornful of athletes who allowed their bodies to turn to fat when they retired, and he worked hard to keep himself lean and muscled. Giving a satisfied pat to his flat stomach, he tugged at the cuffs of his shirt until a precise quarter inch was showing. Then he swung around to look at Helen, who was sitting on the edge of the bed. His mouth curled in barely concealed contempt.

"You know what your real problem is, Helen? You've forgotten who's who in this marriage."

"No, of course I haven't —"

He cut across her words. "*I'm* the United States senator, for God's sake! You're a former exotic dancer from a second-rate casino who started out her career as a waitress. A waitress! How could you imagine I would have any interest in hearing your opinion about a complicated subject like bio-weapons research? Or any other political topic, for that matter. It would be laughable if it wasn't so insulting."

Helen dug the palms of her hands into the bed linens, where she could better conceal the tremors. "It's true I was a waitress and a dancer in a casino, but that doesn't mean I can't have opinions on current events. I read the papers and the weekly business journals. I watch news program on TV. And I was pretty smart in high school —"

"Sure you were." Franklin's voice oozed sarcasm. "Which, presumably, is why you ended up working as a waitress. There's a career that takes a real high IQ."

"Being a good waitress requires a lot more skill than you might think. Not to mention that it's incredibly hard work. I earned every nickel of my tips." Helen stopped short. They'd had this conversation before, and Franklin wasn't interested in hearing what he termed her excuses for not going to college. He didn't care that her father had lost yet another job due to his violent temper right as she was graduating from high school, with the result that money had been even tighter than usual in the Kouros household. With her father on unemployment, and making little effort to find a job, she'd given up her dream of going to college. Instead, she'd worked as a waitress to save money so that Philip, her brilliant younger brother, would have the educational opportunities she'd missed. But Philip was yet another touchy subject as far as Franklin was concerned, and so Helen steered away from it.

She drew in a steadying breath. "Franklin, I only want to make our marriage work better. Tell me what I can do to make things right between us —"

"Quit trying to be somebody you're not," Franklin said, striding toward the bedroom door. "Look, I told you already I'm late for a meeting. I don't have time for any more of this stupid discussion. Just keep in mind that if I'd wanted to marry a college professor, I sure as hell wouldn't have gone looking for my wife in the Swansong casino."

That sounded as if he'd been actively looking for a wife when he came to the Swansong, as opposed to being swept off his feet by her charms, which is what he'd claimed had happened. "What do you mean exactly?" she asked.

He made a dismissive gesture, brushing away her question. "I mean that the way you can please me is to keep your opinions to yourself and fix a happy smile on your face whenever you're with me and my friends."

"I've been doing that for two years. My smile is wearing thin."

"Yeah, well, work on it, babe. And while you're at it, find something to wear to the reception tonight that isn't so damn dowdy. Show a bit of tit and ass, for God's sake. That's what my donors are interested in, not your brains. Such as they are." He walked out of their bedroom without waiting for her to reply, slamming the door behind him.

The noise of the slammed door reverberated around the plushly carpeted bedroom. Helen remained seated on the edge of the bed because her legs were too shaky to support her. She stared dry-eyed into space, her stomach churning. The soft, muted gold of the bedroom walls didn't provide its usual solace, and even the drapes with their interesting design of autumn leaves didn't cheer her up. Attractive surroundings were a very poor substitute for a friendly husband and a happy marriage, she reflected bleakly.

She'd been so excited and hopeful for the first six months of their marriage, determined to justify her decision to marry for security rather than passion. The freedom from a demanding work schedule had afforded her the time to read voraciously, and she'd been thrilled when Franklin had given her a charge card for one of Denver's most prestigious stores and told her to buy a new wardrobe. She was feminine enough to have enjoyed every minute of shopping for the clothes and accessories that she hoped would be part of the magic act that changed her from Helen Kouros, casino dancer, into Helen Gettys, poised and elegant wife of the junior senator from Colorado.

Then there had been the pleasure of transforming Franklin's eight thousand square foot mansion in Cherry Hills into a home that was less garish and more welcoming. She studied every home decorating magazine she could lay hands on, spent hours in the public library researching theories of interior design, and toured furniture galleries searching for ideas. Franklin gave her permission to make whatever changes she pleased, and she strove to do him proud with a makeover that was both tasteful and pleasing to the eye.

She'd taken down the stiff draperies with their pouffy valences and tasseled tiebacks, substituting colorful linens that complemented the bright skies and almost permanent sunshine of the Denver area. She painted the stark white walls in soft, muted pastels to make the overall effect more tranquil, and warmed the main reception rooms by adding area rugs to the slate tiles and polished parquet floors.

She'd worked hard to keep her redecorating costs down and Franklin had never complained about the bills, giving her a false illusion of partnership in the marriage. But he'd never complimented her on the new decor, either, and she'd come to the conclusion months ago that her efforts to turn the house into a home had never especially pleased him. He was not a man who paid much attention to his surroundings, so provided she kept herself busy, didn't attempt to get involved in his public life and was available for sex whenever he slept at home, he didn't much care what she did with the rest of her time.

Helen could almost laugh at her naiveté when she remembered the dreams she'd harbored about the life she would lead when she became Franklin's wife. She wasn't just going to be a perfect mother to their beautiful children, she was going to transform herself into his political partner and become a brilliant hostess as well. Best of all, she was going to be secure. No more teetering on the brink of the financial abyss; no more emotionally draining struggles to keep her brother safe and hold her family together.

She'd imagined hosting intimate little dinner parties in their lovely dining room — dinner parties that would become the high point of Denver's social scene, with all the local luminaries competing for invitations. She'd daydreamed about entertaining Franklin's political colleagues, as well as local business leaders and interesting people from the world of music, theater and the arts.

The intimate little dinners never happened, of course. She had no idea what sort of parties Franklin threw when he was in Washington, but here in Colorado he limited his entertainment to big cocktail parties, with hired caterers, plentiful booze and so many guests that nobody ever actually had a chance to talk to anybody else. Which was probably just as well, since Helen was instructed before every event that she was to keep her mouth shut except to smile. This morning's instruction about finding a revealing dress wasn't a new one, either. Franklin wanted people to notice his wife, but not for her warm personality or interesting ideas.

The sad truth was that she and Franklin had shared a relationship for the past year that barely deserved the name of marriage, but this morning's argument had still caught Helen off guard, revealing the full, sordid depths of the chasm between them. She forced herself to acknowledge reality: her marriage to Franklin Gettys, United States senator from Colorado, was a hollow sham, held in place by a rancid glue of threats and fear. Whatever she and Franklin had hoped to find in each other when they exchanged vows two years ago had long since vanished. The only question that remained was what she proposed to do with the rest of her life.

She would suggest to Franklin tonight that they should seek professional marriage counseling, Helen decided. She'd made the suggestion before and been scornfully rejected, but it was the only hope she could see for building something worthwhile out of the ruins of their current relationship. And what if he refused yet again? She drew in a long, slow breath. If Franklin refused to participate in counseling, she saw no alternative except to file for divorce.

Divorce was an ugly, frightening word, and Helen recognized that she wasn't nearly as strong a woman right now as she had been when she and Franklin married. Two years of listening to her husband tell her that she was ignorant and not very sexy had taken their toll. But she comforted herself with the knowledge that she'd managed to take care of herself since she was eighteen, and she could surely take charge of her life again if she set her mind to it. She wouldn't allow Franklin's constant put-downs to intimidate her into believing she was no longer capable of supporting herself financially. As for her appearance . . . well, Franklin complained all the time that she had no taste in clothes and didn't know how to make the most of what he termed her assets, but she wasn't hopelessly unattractive. Was she?

Almost scared at what might confront her, Helen walked over to the mirror and stared at her reflection. She pulled a face, not nearly as happy with what she saw as Franklin had been with his appearance a few minutes earlier. Her light brown hair was expensively cut and artfully streaked with blond highlights, but her gray-green eyes had lost the sparkle that had been her trademark at the Swansong casino. Her cheeks had no color and she was too thin — a better problem than being overweight, maybe, but she'd always liked the fact that her body was athletically fit rather than fashionably emaciated. She was twenty-eight years old, and the unpleasant truth was that she could only have been mistaken for a woman in her mid-thirties with no problem at all.

Helen turned away from the mirror, invigorated rather than depressed. Improving her physical appearance was surely one of the easiest tasks confronting her. Instead of lamenting that she looked a wreck, she needed to work on getting back the gleam in her eyes and the glow in her complexion. After all, how hard could it be to put on seven or eight pounds? Finding a way to consume more calories was surely a problem most women would love to have!

She grinned, her mood lifting further. She was an optimist by nature, and Franklin hadn't yet succeeded in leeching all the natural exuberance out of her. Later on this morning, she was having lunch with her brother, Philip, at their favorite Italian restaurant in LoDo. She would order ravioli with cream sauce, and tiramisu for dessert. That should make an excellent start on gaining back the missing pounds.

And tonight she'd lay down her ultimatum to her husband. Counseling or divorce. His choice, but it had to be one or the other. She'd finally stopped being a doormat, Helen decided. After two years of trying to transform herself into the meek, subservient slave Franklin Gettys wanted, she was going to abandon that destructive quest and become her own woman once again.

She felt better already.

Chapter Two

Philip was already at the restaurant when Helen arrived. He'd taken advantage of the warm May day to request a table outside on the sidewalk, and he was studying the menu in the shade cast by a brightly-striped awning.

He was looking terrific, she saw with relief. His face had acquired the start of a summer tan, his thick brown hair shone and his huge dark eyes — so much like their mother's — glowed with animation. It was almost a month since she'd seen her brother and he appeared visibly fitter than at their last meeting.

"Hi, Nell, how's it going?" Philip stood up and gave her a quick hug before slouching back into his chair and trying to find somewhere to tuck his feet. He was tall, like her, with most of the length in his legs, and the small ironwork table didn't allow either of them much room.

"I'm fine, thanks." It was automatic for

Helen to present a cheerful facade to her brother. He found his own burdens hard enough to carry, so she never attempted to have him shoulder hers as well. "How about you, Phil? You're looking great."

"I'm feeling pretty damn good, too." He shoved up the sleeves of his cotton sweater, then flexed his arms, displaying a modest set of biceps. "I've been working out, as you can see. In fact, I've been hitting the gym four or five times a week."

Helen squeezed his forearm and rolled her eyes in mock awe of his new muscles. "Wow, I'm seriously impressed!"

"You should be." He flashed her a teasing grin, reminding her that he was heart-stoppingly good-looking when he was healthy. "You can call me Iron Man."

She groaned, but gave his forearm another admiring squeeze. "Schwarzenegger had better look out. You're about to steal his glory."

"Yeah, you're right." Philip's grin deepened. "With a couple of thousand more hours in the gym, I could be serious competition for good ole Arnold." He rolled down his sleeves and handed her a menu. "I'm going to order my own personal pan pizza with extra cheese. How about you? Are you sticking with your usual rabbit food?"

She shook her head. "Today I'm thinking pasta. Lots of pasta."

Her brother turned his thumbs up in silent approval, and tipped his chair back, enjoying the moment. His robust appetite was another positive sign, Helen mused. When he craved a hit, eating was just about the last thing on his mind, and at the height of his addiction, he'd become terrifyingly thin.

Her brother had been clean and sober for two years, ever since he'd checked himself into rehab just after her marriage, but Helen still hadn't forgotten the nightmare period when every phone call had set her heart pounding as she wondered if this was going to be the occasion when the police informed her that Philip had skipped out of the latest residential program and was dead of an overdose.

Helen pushed the bad memories aside and twisted around so that her back was to the sun and she could study the menu. Her heart gave a little lurch when she recognized the man sitting at a window table inside the restaurant. It was Ryan Benton, accompanied by an exceptionally pretty young woman with fluffy blond curls. She felt a spurt of totally irrational resentment of the blonde, which she turned into a silent question. What was Ryan doing in Denver? She hadn't seen him since the night she'd accepted Franklin's proposal, and it was disconcerting to realize how her breathing quickened and her pulse raced at the mere sight of him. It had always been that way when she and Ryan were together. One glimpse was all it took for her body to respond, reacting to some subliminal sexual urge that was all the more powerful because it was primitive, visceral and totally outside the realm of rational analysis.

Unfortunately, an intense physical attraction was pretty much the sum of what she and Ryan had shared. When Franklin had first asked her out on a date, Ryan had been disbelieving to hear that she'd agreed to go with him to a reception at the governor's mansion in Denver. Ryan's disbelief escalated to scorn when she accepted Franklin's offer of marriage a mere eight weeks after that first date.

Ryan had been scathing about her decision but Helen knew that her motivation had been much more complicated than just wanting a rich, successful husband. Even now, with her "sensible" marriage crumbling around her, she still believed that sex, however fabulous and mind-blowing, wasn't much of a foundation for any long-term relationship. Her goals in life had been quite different from Ryan's, and she still believed that you needed shared goals if a marriage was going to work out in the long term. Ryan had been dedicated to his career as small-town sheriff, and she'd yearned to live in a big city and make an impact on the world. He was casual, laid-back, easy going. She was intense, focused, goal-oriented. They hadn't shared any rapport outside the bedroom, and she'd told him as much when he asked her to marry him, a couple of weeks before she started dating Franklin.

"So we'll spend our lives in bed," Ryan had said, slanting her one of the smiles that made her heart melt and her toes curl. He'd wrapped his arm around her shoulders and Helen had felt herself weaken, snuggling against his chest, breathing in the scent of his skin and allowing a blissful sensation of homecoming to wash over her. Then common sense had returned and she'd been angry — with him and with herself. It seemed that Ryan only had to smile his sexy smile and all her own ambitions melted under the heat of his charm. She had never understood why he tempted her so much. She knew from bitter experience that life was a serious business, with difficult challenges waiting to ambush any married couple. How could she face those challenges with Ryan as a husband, when they never did anything when they were together except laugh and have fun? What kind of a basis was that for marriage?

She and Ryan had parted hurt and angry, and her feelings grew more raw, more painful as the days passed. It had seemed such a rewarding contrast when Franklin — *United States Senator Gettys* — asked her out on a date. Unlike Ryan, Franklin had no sense of humor, and they for sure didn't spend much time together laughing or having fun. But Helen had seen that as a plus. She was fascinated by Franklin's references to his work in the Senate, and hypnotized by his casual mention of great national figures like Senator Edward Kennedy, Supreme Court Justice Thomas Clarence and Donald Rumsfeld, the secretary of defense. How amazing it would be to meet such important people face-to-face! Helen had been infuriated by Ryan's sarcastic comment that she needed to blink the starshine out of her eyes so that she could look behind the job title to the man himself. If Franklin Gettys hadn't been a senator, would she still be interested in him, Ryan demanded.

She knew the answer to that question now, Helen realized, suppressing a grimace, although it had taken her much too long to realize the truth. She'd been foolish enough to think that marrying a senator would give her the sense of personal fulfillment she craved. After two painful years of marriage she finally realized that fulfillment could only come from within. A sense of purpose in life wasn't something you could suck in from the outside because your spouse had an important career. You earned fulfillment by your own efforts. She sure had learned that lesson the hard way.

Helen was still staring at Ryan's profile — fortunately he hadn't noticed her — when she felt her brother's hand closing over hers. "What's up, Nell?" he asked quietly. "Not to beat around the bush, you look like hell."

"I do?" Helen gave a wry smile, tearing her gaze away from Ryan Benton and burying the erotic memories deep in the past where they belonged. "And I thought this shade of moss green was especially flattering."

"It's not your clothes," Philip said. "They look great. Very fashionable, as far as I can tell. It's you, Nell. Your eyes have got that look they had right after Mom died. Like you're lost somewhere real unpleasant between sad and haunted."

She was surprised that her brother had noticed anything amiss, partly because she'd always been good at hiding what she was feeling. Mostly, though, she was amazed that Philip had progressed far enough with his recovery that he was finally sensitive once again to the signs of another person's unhappiness. It had to be at least five years since he'd last been sufficiently outward-looking to pay real attention to subtle clues about her mood. Or anyone else's mood, for that matter.

Helen started to protest that she felt fine, just a little tired, then cut off the threadbare lies. If Philip was far enough into recovery to notice when she was upset, he deserved to hear at least a modified version of the truth about her crumbling marriage.

"It's been a rough morning," she said. "Franklin and I had a humdinger of a row, which is something we seem to be doing quite often these days. On the rare occasions when he's home, that is."

Philip held her gaze. "Anything I can help with?" he asked.

She managed a smile, although she was afraid it wasn't very convincing. "Thanks for the offer, but this is something we have to work out ourselves."

"Okay, but I make a real good listener."

He gave a wry grimace. "All those years of expensive group therapy have to be good for something, you know."

Helen was surprised at how badly she wanted to confide in her brother, but habit won out and she shaped a bland response that barely hinted at the details of the morning's ugly scene. "I guess the short version is that Franklin and I have very different views about what it means to have a committed, caring relationship. I'm starting to get a little tired of making excuses and pretending things will work out in the end if I just have patience."

Philip's voice became husky with sympathy. "You've found out about the other women," he said quietly, as if stating the obvious. "I often wondered if I should tell you, and then I decided it wasn't my place to butt in. I'm glad I don't have to keep pretending anymore."

Helen put down the menu and stared at her brother in stupefied silence. What was Philip talking about? What other women? He seemed to be suggesting that Franklin had been unfaithful, not just once, but often.

Philip took one look at her and muttered a curse under his breath. "Damn, I've stepped right into it. You didn't know. You and

Franklin were fighting about something else this morning. Jeez, I'm real sorry, Nell. Forget I said anything."

Her tongue finally unglued itself from the roof of her mouth. "You have nothing to apologize for."

"Yeah, sure I do. I should have made certain we were talking about the same thing before I shot off my mouth. Anyway, I'm probably mistaken." Philip started to talk at random about the menu, the weather and one of the kids he was tutoring at the drop-in center where he worked.

Helen finally cut him off, unable to bear his efforts to pretend he hadn't said what they both knew he'd said. "How do you know Franklin has been seeing other women?" she asked.

Seeing. There was a pathetic euphemism if ever she heard one.

"I know a couple of people who know people," Philip said vaguely, obviously reluctant to be more specific. "Some of the stories filter back to me because I'm your brother, I guess."

At gut level, Helen had depressingly little difficulty in believing that her husband had been unfaithful. But on a more intellectual level, it struck her as unlikely. Franklin counted on the support of conservatives who were big on family and traditional values. He simply couldn't afford to risk alienating such an important part of his constituency. Could he?

"It's most likely just rumors," she said. "Franklin's handsome and he has a friendly manner in a social setting. People might be mistaking ordinary friendship for something more."

"Yes, I expect that's it," Philip said. "You're right. Of course you are. People love to invent gossip and scandals."

His eagerness to agree with her had the perverse effect of convincing Helen that the stories he'd heard had been embroidered with more than enough colorful details to convince him they were true. Her heart started to pound in double time, but she covered her agitation with a rueful smile. "You are one lousy liar, little brother. You don't for a moment think these are false rumors, do you?"

"Here comes our waitress," Philip said, with almost comical relief at the welcome interruption. "I'm hungrier than a hibernating bear. How about you?"

Helen ordered mushroom ravioli, although she was afraid it might choke her if she actually had to eat more than a token mouthful, and added an order of iced raspberry tea. Her brother ordered pizza and Coke.

Their server disappeared back into the restaurant. Ryan Benton, she noticed, had gotten up to leave with his companion. Instead of feeling relief at his departure, the knot of tension in the pit of her stomach tightened. Her emotional system seemed to be totally out of whack, unable to cope with the impact of too many shocks in too short a space of time. There was no justification for her crazy sensation of regret, much less for her sudden yearning to hear his voice again.

Hiding a sigh, she turned her attention back to her brother, ignoring the fact that he looked ready to slide under the table rather than answer her questions. "I know you're hoping I'll gloss over your comment about Franklin's extramarital affairs," she said. "Sorry, Phil, you're out of luck. I need to know the truth. Have you just heard vague rumors about Franklin being unfaithful, or are the stories more specific?"

Philip sent her a wry glance "You're not going to let this subject drop, are you?"

"Absolutely not, so you might as well put us both out of our misery."

Her brother stared into the distance for a few seconds, then spoke rapidly. "I'm good friends with Miranda Parton. She volunteers quite a bit at the center, and I don't think she's the sort of person who likes to spread malicious gossip for no reason."

"Miranda Parton? Isn't she one of Franklin's staffers at his office here in Colorado?" Helen asked. "I remember meeting her once. She seemed competent, and very nice, too."

"She is competent and nice. And, yes, she worked for Franklin in his Denver office."

"But she doesn't work for him anymore?"

"No, she quit." Philip didn't elaborate. "According to Miranda, Franklin has affairs all the time. Not long-lasting affairs and never with his staff. Just weekends in the Bahamas, or a quick ski trip to Aspen, that sort of thing. One of the women she mentioned him being involved with was Natalie Rodriguez."

"I see." Natalie was the weather forecaster for a local TV channel and a minor Denver celebrity in her own right. Trust Franklin to be smart enough to limit his adultery to women who were public figures and not likely to sue him for sexual harassment. Helen took a sip of ice water. "Doesn't it bother Franklin's staff that they're working for a man who preaches family values and yet is consistently unfaithful?"

"It's possible most of Franklin's staff

doesn't realize what's going on," Philip said. "Miranda was responsible for his scheduling so she was bound to notice things that the others didn't."

"Senators have to leave phone numbers where they can be contacted in an emergency. Most of his staffers would surely know if Franklin was spending the weekend in the Bahamas, or escorting a perky ski bunny up to Aspen. Why would they cover for him? Why not leak a juicy story to a hungry journalist?"

Philip shrugged. "Political staff tend to be superloyal, I guess. That's why they're hired in the first place — because they agree with the views of the man they work for."

"And you think staffers who support Franklin's conservative views on family values would remain loyal to him even though he's cheating on his wife at the same time as he's preaching to the media about the sanctity of marriage?"

"Maybe." Philip swirled the melting ice cubes in his glass of water, hesitant to meet Helen's eyes for the first time that morning. "The thing is, Nell, Franklin has spread the word far and wide that you're not willing to participate in his public life and your aloofness annoys his supporters. According to Miranda, he's often hinted that you're not willing to participate in his . . . um . . . private life, either, and so it's possible they make excuses for his sexual adventures on the grounds that you're not an . . . um . . . proper wife."

Helen felt fury bubbling up from deep inside. "Franklin tells people that I'm not willing to play any role in his public life?"

"Well, yes." Philip's eyes narrowed and he looked up from his ice-stirring. "Why are you sounding so annoyed, Nell? You know you hardly ever attend any political functions with Franklin. In fact, I was wondering myself if you would do more with him when he gets geared up for next year's reelection campaign."

It was too humiliating to admit that she wasn't allowed to attend most events because her husband considered her an embarrassment. Recalling how just this morning Franklin had summarily rejected her plea to be allowed to play a role in his political career, Helen fought to keep hold of her temper. The effort not to shout and yell left acid burning in her stomach.

"Franklin's exaggerating," she said with hard-won calm. "I attend quite a few functions with him when he's in Denver." Somehow she managed to sound like a sane person, instead of a foaming-at-the-mouth banshee, which was how she felt. "In fact, I'm going to a huge fund-raising reception with him tonight. I sounded annoyed because I resent the implication that I'm not willing to do my share of handshaking, that's all. I attend every single function that Franklin ever invites me to."

"I can see why the rumors that you're uncooperative would make you mad. I know how friendly and outgoing you are even if Franklin's staffers don't."

Her reaction might be irrational, but Helen was almost more hurt that Franklin had distorted the truth about her willingness to be involved in his career than she was about the fact that he'd been unfaithful. When she recalled the dozens of times she'd begged to be allowed a role in his public life, his pretense that she refused to participate seemed as much of a betrayal as his adultery.

The waitress arrived carrying Philip's pizza still sizzling on a metal platter, and Helen's ravioli steaming in a colorful ceramic bowl. Helen was grateful for the excuse to remain silent during the ritual offering of freshly ground pepper and grated Parmesan cheese. She needed a few minutes to recover her equilibrium.

"Enjoy your lunch!" the waitress said as she dashed off.

Helen stirred sauce into her pasta, giving her brother a decent imitation of a smile. "This smells even better than it looks. I didn't get breakfast this morning, so I'm really hungry."

"Don't, Nell." Philip spoke with sudden forcefulness. "Don't pretend it doesn't matter that the bastard's betrayed you."

Helen stared unseeingly at her meal, then forced herself to swallow a piece of ravioli as an excuse not to answer her brother right away. She gradually absorbed the knowledge that the anger she felt toward Franklin was intense, but it was barely tinged by grief. What a sad commentary on their travesty of a marriage, she thought, that she could contemplate its end with an emotion that felt closer to relief than anything else.

Philip wiped his fingers on his napkin, and rested his hand over hers once again. "Okay, Nell, lecture time. You're looking really down in the dumps, so I'll repeat the advice you've given me a hundred times. Don't blame yourself for other people's bad behavior. You're a good wife to Franklin, and you're not responsible for the fact that he's a lousy husband. The guy's a fool not to realize what a huge asset you could be to his political career, but you aren't to blame for his womanizing. No way, no how."

She smiled, albeit a little wanly. "Thanks for the reminder."

"You're welcome. The doctor is available for consultations any time." Philip took a hearty bite of a second slice of pizza and Helen concentrated for a few minutes on eating enough ravioli to prevent her brother taking her to task.

This was a major role reversal, she thought wryly. If there was any silver lining to the cloud of discovering that her husband had been routinely unfaithful, it would have to be the simultaneous discovery that Philip had his life so much together that he had been able to conceal from her any hint of what he knew about Franklin's adultery. Moreover, he was demonstrating the sort of care and concern for her well-being that she had never before been able to expect from him.

"Divorce him, Nell." Philip spoke into the silence. "I know it's not for me to tell you how to run your life, but you deserve somebody so much better than Franklin Gettys."

She was able to laugh at that, struck by how ridiculous Franklin would find it for anyone to believe that she — the former waitress and casino dancer — deserved a better husband than him — the rich and handsome United States senator. But her brother was right, Helen reflected. She deserved a better husband than Franklin Gettys, and tonight, after the fund-raiser, she was going to tell him so.

Chapter Three

Helen had been smiling with such determination for so long that she was afraid the muscles of her face must be locked in place by now. A portly man, with champagne in one hand and a stuffed artichoke heart in the other, nodded to her in greeting.

She read his name tag and nodded back. "Good evening, Mr. Tazio, thank you so much for coming out tonight despite the rain. I know how much Franklin appreciates your support."

"Great to be here. A good man, your husband. He's right on the money with his insistence that we need taxes cut across the board."

"He will be very pleased to know you approve of his position, Mr. Tazio." Smile glued in place, she moved on.

She greeted the CEO of one of Denver's largest companies, but slipped away before the woman could engage her in conversation. For once, Helen's efforts to avoid speaking to Franklin's guests had nothing to do with his instructions; she simply didn't trust herself to utter anything beyond total platitudes without spewing out some acid comment about her husband that she would later regret. If there was anything she owed Franklin at this point, she thought it might be the dignity of a quiet, hassle-free divorce.

Slipping around a tub of Norfolk pines to escape the CEO, Helen found herself face-to-face with the dean of the Business School at the University of Colorado. Definitely a case of out of the frying pan into the fire. She found her smile again. "Good evening, Professor De Laurens, thank you so much for coming out tonight, despite the rain. I know how much Franklin appreciates your support."

The dean scowled. "I'm not sure your husband's going to have my support for much longer. I don't understand why he continues to endorse massive increases in funding for biological weapons. I've tried to discuss the issue with him on a couple of occasions, and he's just not willing to listen. Your husband can be a mighty stubborn man, Mrs. Gettys."

"Yes, I know he can!" Helen chuckled, as if Franklin were a lovable curmudgeon rather than a narrow-minded bigot. "I've lobbied him about biological weapons, too, professor. I'm hopeful that he'll shift his position before the next election. Just this morning, we were discussing the issue of safety risks, and the problem of protecting stockpiles of biological agents from terrorist attack."

Well, it was true they'd discussed it, Helen thought ruefully, even if Franklin had informed her that she didn't have the slightest clue what she was talking about.

"Protecting the stockpile is one of my major concerns, too," the dean said, looking at her approvingly. "Although I have problems with the ethics of this sort of weapon, as well. We're the most powerful nation in the world, with military technology that's at least five years ahead of the rest of the world. Why would your husband be such a strong advocate of weapons that move us back toward a type of warfare that was condemned as barbaric almost a hundred years ago, at the end of World War I? I'm no pacifist. I understand the need for a strong defense. But we need to be gearing ourselves toward twenty-first century weapons. We need more smart bombs and unmanned planes, weapons that can destroy tactical targets and government buildings. We don't need to be using germ warfare to wipe out innocent populations who are probably more opposed to their tyrannical governments than we are."

"That's exactly how I feel," Helen said, momentarily forgetting that she wasn't allowed to give voice to her opinions. "Believe me, professor, I share your views. In my opinion, the inherent risks of the project outweigh the advantage of high-tech jobs for our state."

"Well, I'm sure you're the most effective lobbyist I could ever have for my cause," the dean said, giving her a quick smile. "How could Franklin possibly resist such a delightful combination of brains and beauty?"

It had been so long since a man had paid her a compliment that it took Helen a moment or two to absorb the praise. Then it registered. The dean of the business school had said she was brainy! Flustered, she was still searching for an appropriate reply when she heard the sound of Franklin's voice, booming behind her.

"Now what mischief are you and my wife brewing up, Thomas?" he asked.

The dean shook hands with Franklin. "No mischief at all. Your charming wife was just assuring me that I can hope for a modification in your position on bio-weapons research before we get to the end of the political year."

"Was she now?" Franklin smiled broadly, but the glance he shot toward Helen was hot with fury. "Well, I can't argue with a lady now, can I? Especially when that lady is my wife." He gave a chuckle that sounded amazingly good-humored, although Helen wasn't deceived. She'd not only disobeyed instructions about talking to the guests, she'd broached the subject of biochemical weapons, which seemed an especially sore spot with Franklin for some reason.

Fortunately, he was too smart to insult her in public. Instead, he half turned so that he could draw forward a man who had been standing slightly behind his left shoulder. She recognized that he was making the introduction to put an end to her conversation with the dean, but nobody else would have realized the motive for his maneuver.

"Helen, honey, this is Ryan Benton. He's not only a detective with our wonderful police force right here in Denver, he's from Silver Springs, where you and I first met."

Her heart started to race and she felt hot color rise into her cheeks. More than two years had passed since she last saw Ryan, and now she'd seen him twice in one day.

"What a coincidence," she murmured,

keeping her gaze fixed firmly on Franklin. "It's a small world, isn't it?"

"Sure is, honey." Franklin beamed at her as if he thought she was the most beautiful, talented woman in the world. He had the politician's knack for displaying whatever emotion he thought would please his audience, and since Thomas De Laurens approved of her, he expressed approval, too. "Ryan, meet my lovely wife, Helen."

Helen had about ten seconds to adjust her expression to one of polite neutrality. "Mr. Benton, it's a pleasure to meet you."

Ryan stepped forward to shake her hand. He was still tall, still lean and he still had thick, light brown hair and hazel eyes, but she knew at once that it was only the physical characteristics that remained the same. The man standing in front of her had lost his easygoing, laughing approach to the world's folly, that much was clear. Next month he would be thirty-five years old, and he looked as if he'd been stripped of any last tiny remnant of youthful indiscretion years ago. It was impossible to imagine this austere-faced man lying in bed next to her, smiling as he suggested that they could spend the rest of their lives right there, in each other's arms.

"Mrs. Gettys is forgetting that we already

met," he said coolly. "We knew each other before she married you, Senator."

"Is that so?" Franklin's gaze narrowed.

"Oh, of course! He was the sheriff of Silver Springs," Helen said hurriedly, hoping her voice didn't shake. "How are you, Ryan? It's been a long time."

"I'm well. Enjoying my job in the big city. How about you, Helen? Is life as Mrs. Franklin Gettys everything you hoped for?"

"Everything and more," she lied, avoiding Franklin's gaze. Despite Ryan's expression of cool courtesy, she could feel tension shooting back and forth between the two of them with such force that she could only assume everyone else would be equally aware of it. She should learn to be more careful of what she wished for, Helen reflected wryly. At lunchtime she'd been yearning to hear Ryan's voice again. Now she wished fervently that she could have avoided this encounter.

"Being a senator's wife is very challenging," she said, with what she hoped was just the right amount of casual sincerity. For some reason, it seemed very important not to let Ryan know what a total screwup she'd made of her life.

"And I'm sure you rise beautifully to all the challenges," Thomas De Laurens said, smiling at her. "You're a lucky man, Franklin, to have such a lovely and intelligent wife."

"So Helen keeps telling me." Franklin laughed to show that he was making a little joke.

"I've been trying to persuade your husband that we need more cops on the beat in big cities," Ryan said, his eyes directed straight at her. "I've been trying to persuade him to throw his weight behind a bill that's currently languishing in the Senate — one that would provide extra funds directly to cities."

Helen looked at her husband because that was safer than continuing to gaze hypnotically at Ryan. "And do you plan to support the bill, Franklin?" she asked.

"I haven't decided," Franklin said curtly, his public good humor wearing thin at the edges. "Obviously I'm proud of the great work done by our Denver police officers, and I know they could use more help. On the other hand, the citizens of this country already shell out too much of their hard-earned money paying taxes to the government. We have to think long and hard before we politicians decide to spend more of John Q. Citizen's money."

"Maybe our government could stockpile

fewer military weapons and use the money to pay for more police officers," Helen suggested. What the hell. She was going to get in trouble anyway, so she might as well say what she really thought.

"Excellent suggestion," Thomas De Laurens said. "You should listen to your wife, Senator."

If looks could kill, the one Franklin shot at her would have been instantly lethal, Helen decided. Without speaking to her directly, or responding to the dean's comment, Franklin put his arm around De Laurens's shoulder and guided him away with the excuse that he wanted to introduce him to somebody from the mayor's office.

Helen was relieved that Franklin had moved on without making a public scene, but she wished he hadn't taken the dean with him. Being left alone to face Ryan Benton came pretty close to the top of her list of activities to be avoided. Not because she expected Ryan to be cruel or sarcastic, despite his earlier coolness. Rather she was afraid of the opposite, that he would be too kind. Right now, she was balanced on such a knife edge of emotional tension that she was afraid kindness might send her flying into the abyss.

She needn't have worried. The two years

since her marriage to Franklin had apparently changed Ryan as much as they'd changed her. In the past, his hazel eyes had always been warm, with laughter lurking not very far beneath the surface. Earlier his gaze had been courteous, if distant. Now his gaze raked over her with a cynicism that was entirely alien to the open and friendly man she'd known back in Silver Springs.

"You're looking . . . elegant," he said finally. "You have that high-gloss, polished look that women only manage to acquire when they're spending a fortune on their appearance."

"You make high-gloss and polished sound like insults."

"I did? I apologize. Believe me, Mrs. Gettys, that was entirely unintentional."

The sarcasm in his voice provoked a welcome flash of anger. Welcome because anger was a much more comfortable emotion than regret. "Did you come here tonight merely to insult me, Ryan, or was there some more worthwhile purpose to your visit?"

"I came to see you," he said. "My sister wanted me to let you know that she's just landed her first dancing role on Broadway. She's in a new musical that's opening at the end of this month, and she says you were her role model and her inspiration, so she owes you big time."

"Becky's landed a job on Broadway! Oh my God, that's such fantastic news!" Helen was so excited she forgot all her inhibitions and worries about how she had to behave now she was Mrs. Gettys. She flung her arms around Ryan's neck and hugged him tight, laughing up at him as if the past two years had never happened. "I always knew Becky would make it. You and your mom must be so proud."

"Not so as you'd notice," Ryan said, his coldness dissolving into one of his once-familiar smiles. "Mom's only spent every day for the past two weeks trying to find the perfect outfit to wear for opening night."

Helen laughed. "Oh, I wish I could be there for opening night. It would be such fun."

"We'd love to have you join us if you can find the time to get away. Becky would be thrilled."

Helen felt a surge of such intense longing that it was physically painful. If only Ryan knew how badly she wanted to accept his invitation, she thought. If only he knew how absolutely impossible it was for her to do something so harmless. What would he say, she wondered, if he realized that in the two years of her marriage, she'd only left Franklin's house in Cherry Hills to attend a few political fund-raisers and to go shopping? All other outings were forbidden, as she'd found out to her cost when she visited the Half Spur last weekend.

She suddenly became aware of the fact that she was still in Ryan's arms and that several nearby guests were looking at them with undisguised interest. Not to mention the fact that she could feel a prickle at the back of her neck that meant her husband was staring at her from across the room. She quickly stepped out of Ryan's arms, the happiness and laughter draining out of her as she transformed herself once more into the "senator's wife."

"What is it?" Ryan asked. "Is something the matter?"

"No, nothing." She found her professional smile again, and flashed it at Ryan. "Will you please tell Becky how delighted I am for her success? I am truly thrilled. I'll be looking forward to reading the reviews."

"Yes, of course." He was retreating as fast as she was into cool formality. Helen tried not to feel regret for the lost moment of intimacy.

"Will you excuse me, Ryan? It's been wonderful to see you again, but Franklin is sending me one of those silent husband-and-wife messages to please come and rescue him. I have to go."

Ryan's expression took a step further toward polite neutrality, and he inclined his head in an impersonal parting gesture. "The senator is lucky to have you available for rescue duty. Goodbye, Helen. See you in another couple of years, maybe."

"Or sooner I hope." She smiled blindly and walked away, wondering if he had even the faintest clue what it had cost her to produce that seemingly casual parting remark.

Chapter Four

In contrast to his fit of temper that morning, Franklin wasn't in an especially bad mood as he got ready for bed. The fund-raiser had been successful, adding a welcome hundred thousand dollars to his campaign coffers, and his speech had been well received. Basking in the afterglow of the applause and the compliments, his tone of voice was quite mild as he listed Helen's misdemeanors. Confident that she would be suitably submissive, he didn't even bother to check that she was paying attention as he wandered back and forth between the walk-in closet and the bedroom, sipping at a small snifter of brandy as he undressed.

Helen discovered it was almost soothing to let Franklin ramble on now that she had no interest in pleasing him, or putting things right between the two of them. Listening with less than half her attention, she occupied herself nipping off dead leaves from a philodendron plant she had placed to catch the morning sun in the deep bay window. It was hard to take Franklin's complaints seriously when his chief gripe seemed to be that she refused to dress like a bargain-priced whore. She wondered why in the world she had ever felt obligated to please a man who wanted her to display her breasts as a come-on for political donors.

Helen wrinkled her nose in silent disgust, waiting for her husband to pause so that she could get a word in edgewise. When she finally had an opening she spoke quickly, before he could start droning on again.

"Franklin, I want a divorce."

He swung around to stare at her in mute astonishment. He'd just taken off his shoes and he stood on one foot, with a black dress sock dangling from his hand, frozen by shock. His expression couldn't have been more amazed if he'd discovered a space invader with a deadly ray gun standing beside his bed.

"A divorce?" he said finally, as if he'd never heard the word and didn't understand what it meant. "What are you talking about?"

"I want a divorce," Helen said. "I'm sure you do, too —"

His shock gave way to anger. "What the hell have you been smoking? How dare you ask for a divorce? Have you lost your mind?"

"On the contrary," she said with amazing coolness. "I believe I've just come to my senses —"

"It sure doesn't sound like it! If you want a divorce, you need to see a mental health specialist! You're obviously too messed up to know when you have it easy!"

She shrugged, refusing to be intimidated. "Seriously, Franklin, when you think about the time we've spent together over the past eighteen months, we've barely had a single pleasant conversation. You're disappointed in me as a wife and, to be honest, I'm disappointed in you as a husband. The truth is, our views about marriage don't mesh too well."

She didn't specifically mention his infidelity, perhaps because Franklin's extramarital affairs were merely the final prod that had pushed her over the edge. They were a symptom of everything that was wrong with their marriage rather than the root cause of why she wanted the marriage to end.

Franklin balled his sock and tossed it in the direction of the laundry hamper, the action full of suppressed fury. He stormed across the room, his arms outstretched and his hands fisted. Helen jerked back, becoming aware of the fear lurking just beneath her calm facade. She licked her too-dry lips, and realized she was vibrating with tension. She had been psyching herself up all evening to tell Franklin that she wanted a divorce, and she'd dreaded the possibility that he would lose control. Franklin had never been physically abusive, but she'd been worried for months that the potential for violence was there, only a fraction beneath the surface.

His lips tightened when she flinched, but whether in annoyance or because he felt guilty about his aggressive gestures, she wasn't sure. He drew in a harsh breath, seeming to fight for mastery of his surging temper.

"You're not being reasonable," he said finally. "Why would you want a divorce? Do you remember what you were doing when I met you? For Christ's sake, do you remember what a hard, miserable life you were leading?"

She shook her head. "That's your perspective, Franklin. I didn't find my life hard or miserable. I love to dance. I enjoyed every minute of my work at the Swansong Casino —"

"I made you the wife of a United States senator, for God's sake! I gave you credit cards so that you can buy whatever clothes you want. Your financial future is secure —"

"My future is empty," she said flatly, noticing that Franklin mentioned money, but not companionship, much less love. "You won't let me play any role in your life —"

"This is about the fact that you want to have children, isn't it? You're starting that damn fool argument again."

"No, far from it." Helen shook her head vehemently. "This has nothing to do with my desire to have children one day. In fact, the last thing I want right now is to complicate our situation by getting pregnant. This isn't a ploy on my part to change the terms of our marriage —"

"Then what is it?"

"A courtesy to you," she said quietly. "I want to be upfront with you about my plans. I'm going to see a lawyer tomorrow and find out what steps I need to take to get a divorce. You don't have to worry about negative publicity. I promise I won't say anything to the media except that we remain good friends."

In retrospect, she could only be thankful that Franklin had always been so adamant in his refusal to start a family. If they'd had a child, the decision to end their marriage would have been infinitely more complicated. As it was, the only lives that would need to be pieced together again were hers and Franklin's, which meant that the divorce would be painful, but not shattering for some innocent child caught in the middle of an adult disaster.

"I'm not willing to give you a divorce," Franklin said curtly. He took a monogrammed dressing gown from his closet and tied the tasseled belt with a vicious tug, seeming to feel that he needed to be clad in more than underclothes and a single sock in order to give weight to his words.

"But why not?" she asked, bewildered. "We're hardly ever together, and when we are, we fight. You can't possibly be happy with our relationship, Franklin."

"It suits me well enough," he said tersely.

"How can it? You complain all the time about how incompetent I am —"

"I'm not complaining. I'm trying to educate you, so that you can play an effective role as my wife."

"What role is that?" Her bewilderment was tinged with exasperation. "For Heaven's sake, Franklin, face reality. You have more of a relationship with your office assistants than you do with me!"

"What has that got to do with anything?" He gave a bark of disbelieving laughter. "If you think I'm going to allow myself to be divorced by a *waitress*, you can think again."

Of course! The lightbulb clicked on and Helen finally understood why Franklin was so resistant to the prospect of ending their marriage. He was furious that *she* was rejecting *him*. In their relationship, he was supposed to be the person who called all the shots and his opposition to the idea of a divorce was knee-jerk rather than reasoned. With luck, by tomorrow morning he'd be sighing with relief at the prospect of getting rid of a wife who'd proven so inadequate to his needs.

"I don't want to make things difficult for you," she said truthfully. "I'll find a discreet lawyer, and I'll tell him we want to file on the grounds of irretrievable breakdown of the marriage. I won't even tell the lawyer about your affairs —"

"What the hell are you talking about? What affairs? You know how dedicated I am to the values of clean family living. Who's been stuffing your head full of garbage about me having affairs?"

"There's no point in lying," she said, too disgusted to be angry. "I know you haven't been faithful, Franklin."

His face suffused with angry color. "Have you been following me?" he demanded. "Have you hired a private detective to spy on me? Is that why you went out to the Half Spur over the weekend?"

What in the world did the ranch have to do with their divorce? What bee did Franklin have buzzing around in his bonnet in regard to the Half Spur? "No, of course I haven't hired a detective —"

"Then don't leap to conclusions that aren't justified," he said.

"My conclusions are entirely justified." Helen still felt more weary than angry. "You can't keep taking women on vacations to the Caribbean, or up to your ski lodge in Aspen, and expect to keep your activities a permanent secret."

"The fact that I need a break from my demanding schedule doesn't mean I've been unfaithful —"

"Don't." She held up her hand, warding off his lies. "It so happens that Miranda Parton is an old friend of my brother's, and she confided the truth about why she'd left her job —"

"Because she was fired for incompetence," Franklin barked, but he gave a guilty start at the mention of Miranda's name. "Your brother needs to learn to keep his nose out of other people's business," he added.

"And you need to learn to keep your fly zippered if you're going to continue raking in the cash from all your conservative, family values friends," Helen shot back.

He stared at her in mute bewilderment, reminding her of what a doormat she'd been for the past two years. Unable to cope with a wife who answered him back, he gave up on his protestations of fidelity and changed the subject.

"You're not going to walk away from this marriage with any of my money, in case you have dreams of a fat alimony settlement. I trust you haven't forgotten you signed an ironclad prenup —"

"I hadn't forgotten. I don't care about your money, Franklin. I just want out of this sham of a marriage."

He was silent for a couple of minutes while he finished his brandy, and when he spoke again his manner was surprisingly conciliatory. "You're determined about this, aren't you?"

"Yes. Our marriage has been over for months." In any real sense, there had never been a marriage, Helen thought sadly. She gave a tiny sigh, full of regret for the might-have-beens. "Getting a divorce just makes the truth of our situation into a legal reality."

"I guess you're right," Franklin said slowly. "You're not the woman I thought you were when we married, so it's best if we end it. You've been a real disappointment to me. Totally inadequate for the role of my wife."

Franklin was already heaping the blame for the failure of their marriage on her, but Helen had anticipated that. She was just relieved to see that he was coming around to the idea of splitting up now that he'd gotten over his initial shock.

"Would you be willing to wait until next Friday before you make an appointment with your lawyer?" he continued, sounding almost mellow. "I could free up a couple of hours on Friday morning and we could have an initial consultation together. After all, as you mentioned, we both want to keep this breakup as low-key as possible. You don't want to be fending off the media any more than I do, right?"

"Right." It was one thing for Franklin to accept that divorce was the best choice for both of them, but Helen was mystified by his sudden eagerness to cooperate, even to the extent of coming to the lawyer with her. What was she missing here? Why the heck was he suddenly being so agreeable?

Perhaps he was afraid there were loopholes in the "ironclad" prenup she'd signed, Helen conjectured with a cynicism that was new to her. However, since she had no intention of making a fuss, claiming alimony or generating negative publicity for him, she had nothing to worry about. In fact, it would be in her own interests to cooperate as much as possible because she really didn't want to generate a lot of media attention. She just wanted to leave quietly and get on with rebuilding her life.

"If you think it would be helpful, I'll wait until Friday to start proceedings," she said, opening a drawer and taking out a clean nightgown, anxious to escape to another bedroom. "I'll let you know my lawyer's name tomorrow —"

Franklin spoke quickly. "You haven't chosen an attorney already, then? Or had any consultations about the terms of the divorce?"

"No," she said. "I haven't discussed the possibility of getting a divorce with anyone. I thought you should be the first person to know."

"I appreciate that," Franklin said. "An early appointment on Friday morning with the lawyer would be best for me," he added, his manner oddly abstracted, as if his thoughts were somewhere else.

"Then I'll arrange the appointment for nine or ten," she said.

"Thanks." He registered that she had taken a nightgown from the dresser drawer — by chance she'd pulled out something black and transparent she hadn't worn in months — and his eyes gleamed with sudden desire. "How about one last night of sex before we call it quits?" he asked, his voice thickening.

With difficulty, Helen managed to prevent herself shuddering with distaste. "I'm sorry . . ." No, that was a lie. She wasn't in the least sorry. "I don't think that would be a good idea," she said, her voice carefully neutral.

Franklin's eyes narrowed, but instead of launching into a tirade of abuse, all he asked was where she was going to sleep.

"I planned to use one of the guest rooms. But I could move into a hotel if you'd prefer that," she suggested.

"No!" His reaction was swift and forceful. Realizing that he'd raised his voice, he gave her a conciliatory smile and spoke more softly. "It's silly to waste money on a hotel, and people might gossip. This house is big enough that we never need to speak to each other even if we both continue living here until the divorce is final. We have three guest bedrooms. Pick whichever one you like."

The longer they talked, the more Franklin's reaction struck Helen as completely out of character. She hadn't expected him to feel deep sorrow at the ending of their marriage, but she would have expected him to make everything as difficult for her as he possibly could. Instead, he was being more agreeable than he'd been in months. Why?

She gave a mental shrug, dismissing the question. When you got right down to basics, she didn't really know very much about what made her husband tick. Obviously she'd never understood the first thing about his attitude toward relationships and commitment, or they would never have married.

Relieved and grateful that the divorce had been agreed upon with so little yelling and almost no hurtful recriminations, she said an awkward good-night and headed for the solitude of the most distant guest bedroom, where she cried herself to sleep, mourning the death of their marriage. A marriage, she realized in retrospect, that had never been much more than a wistful dream.

Chapter Five

The phone call from her brother came early on Wednesday evening, while Helen was exploring the contents of the freezer in search of something for dinner. She had no idea where Franklin was, or what his plans were for the night, but she often hadn't known that sort of thing even before they agreed to divorce, so his absence wasn't surprising or bothersome.

She picked up the phone, her attention focused on whether to microwave frozen chicken casserole or lasagna with Parmesan topping. Since she'd decided to gain a couple of pounds, the lasagna was the way to go, she decided.

"Hello," she said, using her hip to close the freezer door.

"Nell? Thank God you picked up the phone." Philip's voice cracked with anxiety. "I'm at the police station in North Denver near 56th Avenue. Please, Nell, you have to get here right away."

Her stomach tied itself into an immediate knot. "What's the problem?" she asked, her voice hard. She couldn't manage to say anything more, or use a more reassuring tone. Why was her brother calling from a police station? *Please don't let him tell me that he's been doing drugs again.*

His hesitation was audible. "I've been arrested for dealing coke," he said finally.

Dealing coke? Helen's stomach plunged. That was a terrifying new departure. Even at the depths of his addiction, Philip had only used, never dealt. She closed her eyes, her hand gripping the phone so tightly that her fingers ached.

"How much coke?" The answer to that would affect the charges her brother was facing.

"I'm . . . not sure."

"You must know —"

"No, I don't. The cops haven't told me. . . ."

That struck Helen as such an obvious evasion she didn't even bother to call him on it. "When were you arrested?" she asked, wondering if Philip found the roster of questions as wearily familiar as she did.

"This afternoon. The cops came to the Youth Center and they had a warrant to search my locker." Philip's voice rose, his panic barely controlled. “Nell, I didn’t do it, I swear. I’ve been set up —”

“Don’t!” she commanded. “Don’t lie and make excuses, Phil. I can’t bear it when you lie.” She’d already had more than enough of that from Franklin and she wasn’t ready to endure more of it from her brother.

“I’m not lying.” His voice lowered with despair. “Nell, please come. You’re the only hope I have right now. Please get here as soon as you can. They say I have to hang up the phone now, but I’m counting on you to straighten out the mess.”

She was sure he was, Helen thought with unusual bitterness. She replaced the receiver in the phone cradle, her stomach cramping with worry and disappointment. For once in her life, she wished she could count on her brother to be there for her instead of the other way around, but that was clearly a fantasy not likely to be fulfilled in the near future. Maybe never.

Helen shoved the lasagna back into the freezer, slamming the door with all the force of her pent-up frustration. She couldn’t believe that only a couple of days earlier she’d been congratulating herself on the giant strides toward total recovery that Philip seemed to be making. Good grief, how in the world had he managed to fake her out so completely? She could usually see right through his efforts at deception.

She went upstairs to the guest bedroom, so that she could freshen her makeup and change out of jeans into something more formal. She'd learned over the years that if she could look well-groomed and neatly put together, she had a better chance of persuading the police to process her brother into a rehab center rather than through the criminal justice system, but she was getting mighty tired of having to manipulate the system on his behalf. Maybe she'd be doing him a favor if she let the criminal justice system take its brutal course, she reflected tiredly.

Tough love was all very well in theory, but hard to put into practice. She'd been mothering Philip for fourteen years — more than half his life — and the habit by now was ingrained. Surrendering to the inevitable, she quickly checked through her selection of suits, choosing one that was a soft shade of gray with a subtle sheen of heather woven into the silky fabric. The skirt was short, too, which was an added advantage, especially when coupled with a pair of high-heeled shoes. Franklin had a fully equipped exercise room in the house, so she still had her shapely dancer's legs, and she was willing to exploit whatever assets she could come up with to help Philip.

What a complete hypocrite she was, Helen mused, shrugging out of her jeans. She wasn't willing to strut her stuff on behalf of her husband, but if flashing a few inches of thigh could improve the mood of the cop who'd arrested Philip, then she was willing to provide him with whatever eye candy she could come up with.

It was amazing that her brother could still deceive her after all these years, Helen thought, flicking a comb through her hair and giving her makeup a final check. She'd really believed him at lunch when he'd told her that he was working out and generally getting his life together. She'd even believed that he was about to resume his studies at medical school. Obviously, she should have known better.

Squaring her shoulders and mentally preparing herself for what was ahead, she grabbed her car keys and headed for the depressingly familiar terrain of yet another police station.

"There's a woman here to see you," Detective Josie Frutt said, setting a paper cup of Starbucks double-espresso on the desk beside Ryan Benton, her partner.

Ryan looked away from his computer, where he'd just pulled up a list of prior arrests on Philip Kouros. "I'm trying to get the paperwork finished on this afternoon's drug bust so I can go home. Who is it? Can somebody else deal with her?"

"It's Helen Gettys. And she's busy reminding everyone that she's married to United States Senator Franklin Gettys, so we'd better all get our butts in gear and pay attention to her."

Ryan frowned, concealing a crazy little shock of desire at the mention of Helen's name. So much for his often-repeated mantra that he was over her. It seemed the mere mention of her name could cause his mind to go blank and his stomach to knot. Ever since the arrest this afternoon, he'd been wondering if she would follow her usual pattern and turn up to rescue her brother. Now he had his answer, and it seemed she was still firmly on the disastrous path of enablement.

Even though he considered Josie a close friend, his past relationship with Helen was something he'd carefully avoided discussing, and this wasn't a good moment to reveal that he knew the sister of the perp — intimately. He disliked lying to Josie, even by omission, but he had no choice unless he wanted the case to be taken away from him. And of course, he didn't want that because handling the processing of Philip Kouros gave him an excuse to exercise his masochism and spend time with Helen. Jeez, he was pathetic.

Josie poked his shoulder. "Hello, earth to Ryan Benton. Mrs. Gettys is tapping her elegant foot, waiting for us to jump to attention. Are you going to deal with her?"

Ryan looked up, his expression schooled to reveal nothing more than mild curiosity. "What the hell is Mrs. U.S. Senator doing here? And why does she want to speak to me?"

"She wants to talk to you because you're the detective working her brother's case."

"Her brother?" Ryan said, as if he didn't understand.

"Yeah. Apparently Philip Kouros is her younger brother."

"Well, that's a surprise." Uncomfortable with deceiving his partner, Ryan pushed away from his desk and rose to his feet, which gave him the excuse he needed to avoid Josie's gaze. "I guess I'd better go talk to her right away or she'll be calling the commissioner to complain about our incompetence."

Josie gave him a friendly thump on the

shoulder. "Keep your eye on the prize, Benton. Mrs. Gettys clearly knows how to make the most of her assets. Not only is she flashing the senator's name, she's flashing her legs, too. She's wearing a skirt short enough to distract any male still breathing."

Ryan managed a carefree grin as he headed toward the reception area, espresso in hand. "Don't worry, partner. Mrs. U.S. Senator is about to discover I'm *real* good at holding my breath."

He'd spoken too soon and much too confidently, Ryan realized when he saw Helen standing by the dusty window in the crowded reception area, the sun shimmering behind her, burnishing her hair with a subtle gold fire. Jesus, she was more lovely every damn time he saw her. At the reception for her husband, she'd appeared in her element, surrounded by people of elegance, power and wealth. Here in the shabby police station, she stood out like a perfect water lily in a pond choked with algae.

Ryan pulled himself back from the romantic imagery. Helen Gettys was not only the brother of a suspect, she was also a married woman, he reminded himself. And not just any married woman: Helen had rejected his offer of marriage only weeks before she became engaged to Franklin

Gettys. That put her triple-time off-limits and Ryan didn't believe in wasting valuable time fantasizing about a woman who was unattainable. He had once been a starry-eyed country bumpkin, but Helen herself had cured him of that. Nowadays he was strictly big city sophisticated. He liked his women uncomplicated and uncommitted, with no emotional baggage to get in the way of hot sex and the occasional friendly date for dinner and the movies.

Still, it required more effort than he cared to acknowledge for Ryan to drag his gaze away from Helen's entirely amazing legs and focus on her face instead. Not a significant improvement, he discovered, since he should have remembered that she had the most ravishing eyes he'd ever seen, and at the moment they were clouded with worry. To his chagrin, the sight of that worry provoked an urge to protect her — which for sure wasn't an emotion he cared to feel toward a woman who had rejected him in favor of a man whose chief qualification as a husband seemed to be the fact that he had scads of money.

Get a grip, Benton. You're not the first man to discover that women like rich men better than poor ones. Time to stop drooling over Helen's unavailable attractions and concentrate on the all-too-real crimes of her brother.

Ryan had learned over the years that adopting a low-key, laid-back attitude often lulled suspects and witnesses into a sense of security that produced valuable results when building a criminal case. He saw no reason to change this assessment just because he'd spent some of the most amazing moments of his life in bed with the woman he was about to interview.

Adjusting his expression to display nothing more than bland courtesy, he crossed the room to Helen's side. It was disconcerting to discover that the closer he got, the harder he had to fight the urge to wrap his arm around her too-thin frame and assure her that everything was going to be fine.

Which it almost certainly wasn't.

He halted while he was still a couple of feet away from her. "Helen." He held out his hand, and she shook it quickly, giving him a smile that appeared warm, sweet and a little hesitant, just as she'd looked two nights earlier at the god-awful reception for her husband that he'd been dragged to by the chief of police. Ryan's heart skipped a beat, before he reminded himself that Helen had been married to Franklin Gettys for over two years, and Gettys was a consummate politician with vaulting ambitions. Helen seemed thrilled to assist her husband in any way she could. She probably had a morning exercise routine that included ten minutes of practicing sweet, innocent smiles in front of the bathroom mirror.

Ignoring his thumping heart, he returned her smile with a cool nod. "I wondered if you'd come to your brother's rescue," he said.

She looked away, not responding to the implicit rebuke in his words. Before Franklin Gettys arrived on the scene, the only subject they'd ever argued about had been her overprotective attitude toward her brother.

"I didn't realize you worked in this precinct," she said.

"I've been here ever since I left Silver Rapids, which was two years ago."

"I thought you despised big city police departments after your experiences working with the Denver police ten years ago. I thought you always wanted to work in a small town. I seem to remember you told me that you'd be quite happy to be town sheriff until the day you retired."

"Circumstances change, and people, too." He'd left Silver Rapids in something mighty close to a temper tantrum after she'd rejected him. He'd come back to bury his hurt in the brutally hard work of being a big city cop only to discover that he actually preferred being at the center of the action. But Ryan didn't want their conversation to start wandering down dangerous byways into the past, and he brought her back to the present with brusque efficiency.

"You've probably been told that I'm the detective assigned to your brother's case. I executed the search warrant at the Youth Center this afternoon."

"I didn't know that until I arrived here," she said softly. "Philip didn't tell me when he called."

She sounded sad and tired and . . . lonely. Annoyed with himself for reading way too much into her words, Ryan held open the door to an interview room and gestured for her to go inside. It was disconcerting to discover that after so many years in law enforcement, he was still having such a hard time separating his personal feelings from his job responsibilities.

"We can be more private here than at my desk. Can I get you a cup of coffee? We have bottled ice water, too." He made the offers mechanically, concentrating on getting back into investigative mode. Think Mrs. Franklin Gettys, he lectured himself. Think *married woman.* Forget Helen Kouros, sleepy-eyed and sexy in his bed. That woman didn't exist anymore.

"No, thank you." Helen sat down, crossing one exquisitely long leg over the other. Ryan gulped and directed his gaze to an unattractive black smear on the wall above her head, staring as if he'd never seen it before, although in fact it had been there for at least a year. He wondered if Helen realized that the prim neckline on the jacket of her suit made the short skirt even more eye-catching than it might have been in a more blatantly sexy outfit.

Of course she realized, he thought cynically. This was a woman who'd captivated the attention of every man working at the Swansong Casino — and been the most popular dancer with customers, too, even though she had no professional training and got by on charm and vivacity rather than expert dancing technique.

Shape up or ship out, Benton, he warned himself. He needed to pull himself together or take himself off the case if he couldn't keep focused on the facts of Philip's crime rather than the attractions of Philip's sister. He cleared his throat. "What information do you want from me, Helen?"

She got straight to the point. "My brother called and told me he'd been arrested on a drug-dealing charge . . . that you found cocaine in his locker at the Youth Center. What exactly are the charges? And what grounds do the police have for believing that my brother has been dealing drugs?"

"We received a tip-off yesterday that your brother was using his work at the Center as a cover for dealing drugs," Ryan said, choosing his words carefully. "Specifically that he was dealing cocaine in large quantities. Since there are a lot of at-risk young people who use the Center as a supposedly safe place to hang out, we obtained a search warrant immediately, and I searched the premises with the assistance of two uniformed officers. Drugs were found in your brother's locker, inside a small duffel bag that he identified as his." He paused for a moment, then gave her the bad news. "We found almost five hundred grams of cocaine, Helen —"

"Five hundred grams!" she exclaimed. She sounded appalled, which was no surprise. She had enough experience with drug busts to know that five hundred grams equaled more than a pound of cocaine. Far too much for Philip to claim it was strictly for his personal use, and more than enough to get him convicted of drug trafficking charges.

"My God! Where did Philip get his hands on such a huge amount of coke! How could he even pay fo—" She broke off, realizing that sounding horrified wasn't the best way to help her brother. "What did Philip say when you confronted him with the stash of coke?" she asked, recovering her composure.

"He said he'd never seen it before," Ryan replied, not bothering to conceal his cynicism. "He said he'd been set up."

Helen dropped her gaze to her lap. "Philip might be telling the truth . . . . How can you be sure the drugs weren't planted?" Her voice wasn't steady, and Ryan was quite sure she didn't believe her brother's claims of innocence any more than he did. They both knew Philip was an addict with a long history of cocaine use. He wished he didn't have to confirm her fears, but Philip was following a depressingly familiar pattern, even if he was the brother of the woman Ryan had once loved and wanted to marry.

"It's difficult to imagine how the drugs could have gotten into your brother's locker without his consent," Ryan said. "There are heavy-duty combination padlocks on all the staff lockers at the Center. The padlock on

Philip's locker was intact, which means whoever put the drugs there didn't have to break it to gain access. If the lock hasn't been tampered with, and it's your brother's locker, he's not just the logical suspect. He's the only suspect."

"Maybe he didn't adjust the combination dial on the padlock to close it properly —"

Ryan shook his head, not allowing her false hope. "The lock's self-closing."

"But you must need to click it. Philip might have forgotten to click it shut. Or maybe somebody else at the Center knew his personal access code."

Ryan felt like a brute as he squashed one hope after another. "Your brother himself admitted that he hadn't told anyone the combination for his padlock. We're left with the entirely logical conclusion that Philip put the coke into that bag himself. It doesn't help that he has a long history of problems with drug abuse, and several prior arrests."

"Okay, we both know my brother has a history of using cocaine," Helen conceded. "But you know as well as I do that he's always been a user, not a dealer. I swear he's never, ever dealt drugs before. Not when we knew each other, or since." She leaned forward, pleading her brother's case with passionate intensity. Ryan repressed the urge to go find Philip and beat some sense of remorse into his airy, coke-filled head.

"You know Philip was a medical student, one of the most brilliant in his class, before his drug use got the better of him. He's always been really conscious of not wanting to facilitate anybody else's habit. I know my brother, and I can't believe he'd start dealing. No way, no how."

Ryan refrained from quoting the horrifying statistics on nurses, surgeons and other medical specialists who had problems with drug addiction. "The fact that your brother didn't deal in the past doesn't mean much," he said quietly, hiding his frustration at her ongoing reluctance to face up to the reality of her brother's addiction. "Using cocaine exacts a heavy toll on a person's moral standards, Helen —"

"But he hasn't been using anything for months, I swear!"

"Remember we got a phone tip that he was dealing," Ryan said shortly, feeling all his old frustration rebuild, although whether with himself, with Philip or with Helen he wasn't sure. "We're not just basing his arrest on the fact that we happened to stumble across the coke in his locker."

"Do you know who the tip came from?"

"No," he admitted. "But that doesn't mean anything. Tips about drug deals usually come from clients who've fallen out with their suppliers and we expect them to be anonymous."

"So you think the tip came from one of Philip's . . . drug clients?"

He nodded and she turned abruptly, hiding her eyes, but Ryan could tell that she was deeply distressed. Whatever else might have changed about Helen Gettys, it was clear that she still cared a lot about her younger brother. Probably too much for Philip's own good. The kid might have done better without a supportive sister to come running every time he screwed up.

"My recommendation is that you hire a good lawyer," Ryan said when she didn't speak. "Your brother is facing charges that could buy him serious jail time. But you know that already, I'm sure."

"My brother doesn't have any money."

He was surprised by her response. "Well, maybe not. But I assumed you would be hiring the lawyer on your brother's behalf."

"Oh. Yes, of course." She looked down at her hands, which were clasped in a death grip in her lap. When she looked up again, he saw that her face had lost every trace of color and she was biting her lower lip in an effort to keep it steady. She made no further reference to his comment about hiring a lawyer.

"I'd like to see my brother, please."

"Are you planning to bail him out?"

Her pallor vanished, replaced by a wash of crimson. She was clearly embarrassed, but he couldn't pinpoint the source. As an investigator, he wasn't doing too well in assessing what made Helen Gettys tick. Fact was, he was having a real difficult time separating his memories of Helen Kouros, naked in his bed, and Helen Gettys, sophisticated wife of Colorado's junior senator.

"I'm . . . not sure if I'll bail Philip out," she said. "But I definitely want to see him. I really need to talk to him and find out firsthand what happened today."

Her beloved kid brother had been caught dealing cocaine, that's what had happened today. Ryan suppressed a sigh. It seemed that Helen was still acting the role of enabler, a role he'd tried to persuade her to abandon years ago. She would try to extract a promise of reform from her brother before agreeing to bail him out. Ryan debated telling her that she would be a complete sucker if she believed her brother's promises, or fell for his likely excuse of having been set up by some unknown enemy, probably the cops. He decided to save his breath. He and Helen had been down that same frustrating road too many times already and there was no point in going there again. Philip Kouros was a smart guy and an addict, which meant by definition that he had a real good line in stories that blamed everyone in the universe for his problems except himself.

"I'll arrange to have you escorted to the holding cells," Ryan said, getting to his feet to prevent himself getting dangerously involved. "Goodbye, Helen. I'm sorry that we had to meet again under such unpleasant circumstances."

She acknowledged his remarks with nothing more than a brief nod of her head, but even though seeing her again had messed with his head to the point that his emotional radar was almost nonfunctional, Ryan understood that she wasn't being standoffish. He realized she was simply holding herself under tight control for fear that she would fall apart if she relaxed even a tiny bit.

Stifling a rush of sympathy that there was no appropriate way for him to express, Ryan turned sharply, anxious to escape from a situation that offered no good outcome for either of them. Helen was married, her brother was an addict and he was a cop. Three points of a triangle with no good way to connect the dots, especially in view of their past, failed relationship.

"Wait here," he said, suppressed emotion making his voice curt. "I'll send a uniformed officer to escort you to the cells."

"Thank you." Her voice was husky. "I appreciate your help, Ryan."

"You're welcome. I'm sorry I happened to be the one to make the arrest." It seemed an inadequate response, but it was all he could offer her. He left the interview room without looking back.

Whether because Ryan had taken pity on her and pleaded for special consideration, or else because the cops were impressed by the fact that she was the wife of Franklin Gettys, Philip was locked in a holding cell by himself, and Helen was allowed to go inside with him.

She entered warily, keeping her distance. "Hi, Phil. How are you doing?"

Her brother didn't rush over to hug her, or even thank her for coming. Standing in the corner of the cell, fists clenched, he spoke with low-voiced passion.

"I didn't do it, Nell. I've been set up."

Her temper, rubbed raw by the events of the past few days, snapped. "Oh for goodness sake! For once in your life can't you just take responsibility for what you've done? Ryan's a decent man and a great cop. Why would he arrest you unless he had real cause?"

Philip glanced down at his scuffed sneakers. "I deserve that," he said quietly. "I know I let you down a lot of times in the past. But not this time."

"You're in jail, charged with dealing cocaine. You haven't just let me down, Philip. You've let yourself down."

Her brother's voice deepened, throbbing with urgency. "I didn't do it. I haven't done any drugs in almost two years, since just after you got married. I haven't even had a beer. I'm stone-cold sober and have been for months." He walked across the cell and grabbed her by the arms. "Look at me, Nell. For God's sake, *look at me!* You know what I'm like when I'm using. *I'm not using.* Check it out for yourself. You have to believe me."

Helen finally forced herself to meet her brother's gaze in critical assessment. His eyes were clear and focused, she saw, although his body vibrated with a toxic combination of despair, rage and tension. His nostrils weren't inflamed, and his nose wasn't dripping. For the first time since she'd received his phone call, she allowed herself a tiny flicker of hope. Was it possible that the cops had made a mistake? That Ryan had jumped to conclusions based on his prior knowledge of her brother's problems with drug addiction? If Philip really was innocent, she felt she could cope with all the rest.

"The drugs were in your duffel bag inside your locker," she said, not allowing herself to overlook facts despite her desperate wish to believe in his innocence. "According to Ryan, the padlock hadn't been tampered with, and you admitted that nobody else knew your combination number. How did the drugs get inside your duffel bag if you didn't put them there?"

"I didn't speak directly to Ryan," Philip said. "And the cops are either deliberately misrepresenting what I told them, or they weren't listening closely enough. Kids often stand around talking to me when I'm at my locker. It's true that I'd never *told* anyone what the combination is for my padlock, but it wouldn't have been all that difficult for someone to watch me open the lock and take a mental note of the number sequence."

"Did you explain that to Ryan?" Helen asked.

He shook his head. "I told the uniformed

cop who found the coke, but not Ryan. I think since Ryan knows me he wanted another cop to take my statement. But the bottom line, Nell, is that it wouldn't be hard for somebody to have gotten into my locker and plant those drugs."

"But why would anybody want to set you up?"

Philip shrugged, not interested in a question that he found irrelevant. "Could be any one of a dozen reasons. Maybe the real dealer got a tip-off the cops were coming and needed somewhere to hide his stash. Maybe some kid is pissed off at me and I don't know it. Maybe some cokehead zoned out and shoved his supply into my locker by mistake —"

"This mythical cokehead was too zoned out to remember where his own locker is, but he remembered your combination?"

Philip grimaced. "Weirder things happen when you're high. All I know for sure is that I was the unlucky bastard who got stuck with a damn great bag of coke I'd never seen before in my life."

His explanations were all reasonable, but her brother had a stratospheric IQ. How difficult would it be for him to invent credible lies? Helen held his gaze, willing him to be truthful. "Phil, I want to believe you, but it's hard, given what's happened in the past. Tell me one more time. Do you know anything at all about these drugs and how they came to be in your locker? In the long run, it's going to be better for everyone if you tell the truth."

He spoke with fierce intensity. "I know nothing about the drugs, except that somebody else put them in my locker." He smiled bitterly. "You want to hear something funny? I was so damn certain I had my drug problems under control that a couple of months ago I reapplied to medical school. The University of Colorado accepted me to start in January, giving me three semesters of credit for the courses I've already taken. I've even got the financing worked out."

Helen stared at her brother, momentarily speechless. "Oh my God, that's wonderful!" She pulled him into a bear hug, tears clogging her throat. "Congratulations! Why didn't you tell me, Phil? I'm so thrilled for you."

"I was saving the news for my birthday next weekend." He attempted to give a casual shrug and failed miserably. "Well, I guess today's events take care of my chances of ever starting medical school again."

"We won't let it ruin what you've worked for," Helen said fiercely. "We'll beat these charges, Phil."

"How?" he asked simply. "Even you assumed I was guilty."

"That was before I spoke with you."

Philip gave her a pitying look. "The cops aren't going to be persuaded because I talk a good game. They have all the evidence they need. A tip-off recorded on the drug hotline. A plastic bag stuffed full of high-grade coke and a witness who's willing to swear I sold drugs to his friend. I don't think my protestations of innocence are going to win the day, especially since Ryan Benton thinks I've talked myself out of trouble way too many times already."

"There's a witness to you making drug deals?" Helen's stomach gave another lurch downward. "What's his name?"

"Shawn Johnson. He's one of the few kids at the Center that I don't like. He'd sell his grandmother for a hundred bucks, and his mother for fifty, so his word is basically meaningless."

"What does that mean?"

"It means Shawn has been bought. Still, with my record what hope do I have of convincing the cops I was set up?"

She frowned in thought. "We have to find out who persuaded Shawn Johnson to provide false testimony. Once we have a lead, I bet Ryan would follow up on it. He was always conscientious to a fault when I knew him in Silver Springs."

"That's a great plan," Philip said wryly. "The concept's terrific. Unfortunately, I can see a couple of problems with the practical details. Such as how the hell we're going to persuade Shawn Johnson to admit that he lied?"

Money would be the quickest way, Helen thought. Unfortunately, she didn't have any of that available for bribing Shawn. A credit card good at a fancy boutique couldn't provide ready cash. "I didn't say it would be easy," she said, hiding her worry. "But there must be some way to put pressure on Shawn to give up a name —"

"Yes, we need to bribe him." Philip echoed her thoughts. "The trouble is, I have no money, Nell."

"None?" she asked ruefully, although she wasn't surprised. Working as a counselor at a youth center might be spiritually rewarding, but the pay was lousy.

Her brother shook his head. "I have five hundred bucks in a savings account, maybe another two hundred in checking. That's it. And seven hundred bucks isn't going to buy any useful information from Shawn Johnson."

"Are you sure? That's a fair sum of money for a teenager."

"Yeah, but you have to count in the fear factor. Presumably he was paid off by a big-time coke dealer, which means that telling the truth is going to put him at serious risk of getting beaten up. Or worse. I don't think seven hundred bucks will persuade Shawn to risk dying."

Helen wished with all her heart that she had some money of her own to offer her brother. Quite apart from bribing Shawn to tell the truth, they needed money for a lawyer, and maybe a private investigator. Not to mention bail money, so that Philip could get out of jail while waiting for his trial. Even if they went to a bail bonds outfit, they'd need ten percent in hard cash.

"I'll ask Franklin to loan me the money," she said, sounding a lot more confident than she felt.

Philip shook his head. "No, you won't, Nell. I know damn well that Franklin's forbidden you to give me any money and that he checks all your accounts and bills and receipts to make sure you're not slipping me cash on the side. I'm not going to be responsible for putting you into that man's debt. No way, no how."

"Franklin will understand this is a different situation," Helen said, hoping she was telling the truth. "He disapproves of me giving you money because he believes that earning your own living is an important part of your rehabilitation." That was a somewhat liberal translation of Franklin's edict that she was to stop throwing good money after bad on her no-good asshole of a brother.

"I'll talk to Franklin tonight, and see what we can come up with," she said, determinedly optimistic. "After all, he's a senator. He must know a couple of really top-notch lawyers, don't you think?"

"Probably," Philip said, trying to sound cheerful and not mentioning again what they both knew, which was that Franklin most likely wouldn't be willing to offer any help at all, especially not financial help.

"I really appreciate all you do for me, Nell." Philip ducked his head in awkward gratitude. "Thanks for believing in me one more time. You've done so much for me since Mom died —"

"I'm your sister. Of course I want to help."

"I wish you didn't have to keep hauling me out of trouble. That was one of the worst parts about being arrested this afternoon . . . I hated to disappoint you. I couldn't bear for you to suspect I'd thrown it all away again. I didn't, Nell, I swear."

"I believe you." Helen gave him another quick hug, then stepped back before either one of them broke down. "I'll be back as early as I can tomorrow morning. Keep your spirits up, Phil. We'll straighten out this mess, I promise."

Leaving the police station, breathing in the fresh night air with a sensation of profound relief, Helen could only hope that she'd be able to make good on her promises. First she had to find Franklin. Then she had to persuade him to provide her with a loan of several thousand dollars. A loan that would take months to repay, even after she got a job.

All this when they were about to start divorce proceedings. Plenty of men more generous than Franklin might think twice about helping a wife who was about to apply for a divorce. Especially when the purpose of the loan was to bail out a brother-in-law he'd always despised.

The timing of Philip's arrest couldn't have been worse, Helen reflected, but there was nothing for her to do right now but go home and grovel to Franklin.

She was not looking forward to the task.

Chapter Six

Franklin's BMW was in the garage, suggesting he had come home while she was at the police station. That was a relief, Helen thought. For all she'd known to the contrary, he could have flown back to Washington, which would have made the rescue of her brother a lot more difficult. A sudden image of Ryan Benton sitting across the table from her flashed into her mind. He'd looked so honest and dependable, she thought wistfully. If only she could ask him for help instead of Franklin, she'd be a lot more optimistic that her brother would soon be free.

Dismissing the hopeless wish, she entered the house through the door from the garage into the laundry room. Dropping her purse onto the kitchen counter, she shucked the high-heeled shoes she'd donned to impress the cops. The shoes were new and she wriggled her toes gratefully before setting off in search of her estranged husband.

On the rare nights he spent at home, Franklin liked to watch a sporting event on the TV in his study. Padding along the polished parquet floor of the main hallway, Helen made her way toward the study. She was still several yards from the entrance when she heard the sound of men's voices.

Hoping to find out how long she might have to wait before she could plead her brother's cause, she stopped and listened for a moment, knowing that she would be ruining her chances of success if she interrupted Franklin when he was with a friend or business colleague. The prospect of a long delay was nerve-racking. Truth be told, she was absolutely dreading the discussion and wanted to get it over with as soon as she could.

"It's lousy timing," she heard a man say. "Quite apart from the negative media coverage, we don't want anybody looking over your financial assets right now." The speaker had a distinctive, gravely sound to his voice, and she recognized it as belonging to one of Franklin's most important financial backers, a man called Lio. Helen didn't know Lio's last name, or his profession, but that wasn't surprising since Franklin rarely bothered to make more than perfunctory introductions. All she knew was that Lio must be a close friend as well as a generous political supporter because he came to the house more often than any of Franklin's other associates.

"I'm well aware of the problem," her husband said, sounding defensive.

"Then take care of it." Lio was giving an order, not making a suggestion. How odd, Helen thought. She wouldn't have expected Franklin to tolerate the company of anyone who spoke to him in such peremptory tones.

"I have taken care of it," Franklin replied. "In fact, I wasted most of yesterday dealing with the problem. Trust me, she's going to change her mind about wanting a divorce real soon."

Helen's heart began to beat in double time. Franklin and Lio were apparently discussing her decision to seek a divorce, which was surprising in itself. But even more surprising was Franklin's conviction that she was going to change her mind about wanting out of their marriage. What possible grounds did he have for believing something so unlikely?

Lio spoke again. "Make sure she does back off, Franklin. Things are moving forward at the Half Spur and I don't want any fancy, high-priced divorce lawyers out there poking around —"

"Why would they?"

"Because she'll go after your money and her lawyers will want to find out how much the property is worth in a settlement. I sure as hell don't want anybody to link ownership of the Half Spur to one of my corporations. I've gone to a lot of trouble to hide the fact that you and I are joint owners of the ranch. One nosy divorce lawyer could blow us both out of the water."

"That's not true," Franklin protested. "Helen has no claim to the ranch. She has no claim to any of my assets, for that matter. I've told you before, Lio, we have an ironclad prenup that Helen signed before we ever married."

Lio gave a hoarse laugh. "And I've told *you* before that your prenup isn't worth the paper it's written on. You might as well flush it down the toilet now. Take it from a man who's been divorced three times and is finally smart enough to realize marriage is strictly for losers. There isn't a prenup ever written that can stand up to attack by a lawyer who knows his trade. Besides, in this case it isn't what the judge decides at the end of the day that matters. It's what Helen's lawyers might discover while they're sniffing around, requesting notarized statements from everybody and their dog."

"Yeah, well, we have no worries. Helen isn't going to divorce me."

Like hell she wasn't. Helen resisted the urge to burst into the study and tell Franklin that he was delusional if he thought she was going to change her mind about splitting up. As for Lio, she'd always disliked the man, and his sordid advice to Franklin merely confirmed her bad opinion. They'd sounded like a couple of Mafia dons discussing their illegal business deals, she thought disgustedly.

She heard the sounds of the two men rising from their chairs, the squish of air returning to leather cushions, and the rolling of castors across the oak-plank floor. Very quietly, she turned and ran back to the kitchen. Then she put her shoes on again and emerged noisily into the hallway, creating the impression that she'd just walked into the house.

Her timing was perfect. Franklin and Lio came out of the study at the same time as she *tap-tapped* out of the kitchen. "Why hello, Franklin." She gave him a smile instead of the snarl she'd have liked, and turned to his companion. "And Lio, too. I didn't see your car. It's good to see you again."

"Likewise. My car's around the front." Lio shook her hand, his gaze hot as he made a leisurely survey of her body. She'd learned on previous visits that the man was a letch of the worst type, and she always took care not to be alone with him.

Lio gave her a brief, insincere smile. "Well, I'm sure you and the senator have things to discuss and I need to get home. Take care, Helen."

"Where is your home, Lio?" Helen hoped she made the question sound casual, but she was suddenly very curious about exactly who Lio was and what his relationship was with her soon-to-be-ex-husband.

Lio's eyes narrowed. "I have a home right here in Denver," he said, pausing by the front door. "Goodbye, Franklin." He nodded to Helen. "And you, too. Enjoy your evening."

After Lio had left, Franklin didn't escape back into his study as might have been expected. Instead he turned to Helen with an oddly self-satisfied smile. "Was there anything you wanted to talk to me about?" he asked. "Where have you been at this late hour, my dear? You look as if you're dealing with a crisis."

Franklin's taunting manner, combined with his comments to Lio suddenly made sickening sense. The truth exploded into Helen's consciousness with the force of a rocket launch. Good God, how could she have been so thick-witted for so long? There was no need to go searching for some disgruntled addict to find out who had set Philip up. Her brother was in prison right now because Franklin Gettys had arranged to send him there.

Helen felt as if she might suffocate. She could barely tolerate being in such close proximity to a man who could exploit her brother in such a despicable fashion, but ranting and raging wouldn't get Philip released. With a single furious glare at her husband, Helen turned and stalked into the formal living room. If she'd needed confirmation of her suspicions, Franklin provided it by following her into the room without being asked.

It had to be eighteen months at least since he'd followed her anywhere, she thought acidly. If she'd wanted to capture her husband's wandering attention, it seemed there could be no better method than telling him she wanted a divorce.

Helen walked over to the empty fireplace before swinging around to confront him. "You wanted to know where I'd been. I'm sure you won't be surprised to hear that I've just come back from the police station in North Denver."

Franklin cocked his head in pretense of an

inquiry, but his gloating smile gave him away. "Why would you go there, my dear? A police station isn't a very pleasant place to spend the evening. I do hope you're not about to start off on one of your do-good schemes again."

The endearment set her teeth on edge, but she ignored it. "Okay, let's cut to the chase. What's your deal, Franklin? What do I have to do in order to get Philip out of jail?"

"Your brother's in jail?" Franklin went to the built-in bar, took ice from the automatic ice-maker and poured himself a vodka on the rocks. "What's he accused of this time?"

"Exactly what you arranged for him to be accused of," she said bitingly. "Possession of five hundred grams of cocaine with intent to deal." Franklin started to speak but she cut him off, literally sick to her stomach at the prospect of participating in his cat-and-mouse play.

"I'm not interested in hearing any more of your fake expressions of shock and surprise, Franklin. Let's quit the perverted games and move straight to the bottom line. What do I have to do in order to get the charges against my brother dropped?"

"What makes you so sure that I can make the charges go away?"

Helen's stomach dropped away into the abyss. Had she misjudged? Not that Franklin had set her brother up — she was a hundred percent sure of that. But had her husband set Philip up simply as a form of revenge with no way to spring the trap? Then she remembered Franklin's boast to the mysterious Lio and was somewhat reassured. Her husband had arranged for Philip to be arrested in order to force her to comply with his wishes. That meant there was a way to get her brother out of jail.

"You can make the charges go away if you want to," she said, with more certainty than she felt. "You set Philip up, so I'm damn sure you can spring him. Just tell me the deal, Franklin."

"All right, I will." He took a long swallow of his vodka. "I want you to drop this crazy nonsense about getting a divorce. If you agree that we're going to stay married, I'll do my best to get the charges against your brother dropped."

She shook her head, feeling a hundred years older and wiser than she had been only a couple of days earlier. "No, Franklin, that's not the way it's going to work. First you have to spring my brother from jail and make sure all the charges against him are dropped, and then I'll agree not to divorce you."

The angry look he shot in her direction was tinged with admiration. "Playing hardball, my dear? I didn't expect it from you. But the short answer is, no deal. Who the hell do you think you are, laying down conditions to me?"

She was nearly suffocating with fright, but Helen hid her panic and managed a shrug. "Who do I think I am?" she asked, hoping Franklin couldn't hear the shake in her voice. "Well, I guess I'm the woman you want to keep as your wife. I'm also the woman who can ruin your political career if I decide to do so. All I have to do is give a friendly reporter the details of some of your extramarital affairs, and there goes your support among all the family values folk who helped put you in office."

"You bitch!" Franklin cursed viciously for almost a minute. Helen waited for him to draw breath, then spoke quickly.

"I may be everything you say, but I hold the winning cards on this deal. I'm sure some of the women you've seduced and discarded will be more than happy to go public with their stories, so it's not just my word against yours." She paused for a few seconds to let her threat sink in, then added a threat that she didn't understand, but guessed would be potent. "And if your affairs aren't enough to shake Philip loose from jail, then I'll tell the reporters to take a good look at what's going on at the Half Spur. Now, would you like to reconsider springing my brother from jail?"

Franklin was staring at her as if he didn't know her and she couldn't blame him. Right at this moment, Helen hardly recognized herself.

"You deceptive bitch," he said. "What the hell were you doing out at the Half Spur last weekend? Who sent you there?"

"I was having a picnic," she said, her voice taunting. In other circumstances, she thought it might have been amusing to know that telling the absolute truth could seem so threatening to Franklin's peace of mind.

For a moment she wondered if she'd gone too far. Franklin literally looked murderous. By great good fortune, the phone rang at that moment. She snatched up the receiver and heard a telemarketer offering her a free weekend at a resort in the Rockies.

"Hi, Mary!" she responded, as if the woman were a lifelong friend. "I can't talk right now because Franklin and I are in the middle of a discussion, but I'll get back to you in twenty minutes, okay?" She hung up on the telemarketer in midpitch.

"Are you ready to work out a deal in regard to my brother?" Helen said, turning back to face Franklin.

The phone call had given him time to calm down. "I can get the charges against your brother dropped," he said. "But don't imagine that as soon as he's out of jail, you can renege on our deal and walk away from our marriage. I have cops on my payroll, and the charges against your brother will all come back with a vengeance the day you try to divorce me."

Helen's gaze narrowed. Franklin was obviously desperate to keep her inside the marriage, she reflected, and she would love to know precisely why. What had Lio meant about this not being a good time to subject Franklin's financial affairs to scrutiny? Was he somehow laundering illegal campaign contributions through the ranch accounts? It was the sort of thing she could imagine him doing and it would explain why Lio — probably an illegal campaign contributor — was so anxious to avoid having a divorce lawyer demand to see a statement of the ranch's finances.

There was no chance that Franklin would admit the truth, so she didn't squander her bargaining power — already pretty weak — by asking why he was so desperate to prevent her from seeking a divorce. But she sure as hell planned to use the next few weeks to discover a little bit more about what her husband and Lio were up to, especially at the Half Spur.

"Here are my terms," she said. "I'll keep up the facade of being married to you if that's what it takes to save my brother, but I'm not going to have sex with you ever again, or sleep in the same bed —"

"Is that a threat or a promise?" Franklin asked with heavy sarcasm.

"Neither. It's a simple statement of fact."

"Supposing I say that I want sex, or no deal?"

"Then my brother can rot in jail. There are limits to what I'm prepared to sacrifice for Philip." Helen produced the lie in clipped tones that — she prayed — carried conviction. To her overwhelming relief, Franklin seemed to believe her. Besides, she was sure that his determination to stay married had nothing to do with wanting to keep her as a sexual partner, so it wasn't such a big deal for him to concede. She had no doubt that he'd continue being unfaithful, so he wasn't going to be sexually deprived.

She hit home her point. "I want my brother out of jail by tomorrow afternoon," she said. "Otherwise I'm going to the media with a few juicy stories about the women you've been bedding —"

He grabbed her by the arm, his face turning almost purple with rage. "Don't threaten me," he said. "You were nobody until I made you Mrs. Franklin Gettys, and don't you ever forget that."

She ought to have been frightened by his rage, but it seemed that she'd finally found the backbone that had been missing for the past eighteen months. "I was Helen Kouros before I married you, and she was one hell of a strong woman. I want Philip out of jail. You want me to stay married to you. We've got a Mexican standoff here, but don't ever again make the mistake of thinking you can intimidate me. Get my brother released from jail, or I'll blow you and your cronies right out of the water."

Helen wasn't at all sure that her bluster would work, but for all the shouting that followed, she knew that Franklin had basically surrendered. She decided to back off and act humble, since that was the course of action that seemed most likely to secure her brother's release.

But the humility was an act, even if Franklin wanted to believe that he'd reasserted his mastery. Because if there was one thing Helen was absolutely determined about, it was this. Once her brother was released from jail, she was going to find a way to keep him safe, probably by encouraging him to leave the state. And then she was going to divorce Franklin Gettys.

Chapter Seven

By the time Philip was processed out of the system, Helen was beginning to wish he was less sensitive to other people's emotions, not to mention a lot less smart. Her brother instantly saw through the holes in the story she'd concocted to explain why, thirty-six hours after he was arrested, he was suddenly being released, all charges against him dropped.

Unfortunately, she couldn't risk telling her brother the truth until she had him safely out of the state, far removed from Franklin's reach. If Philip guessed that Franklin was blackmailing Helen to stay married, he might feel compelled to fight for justice by remaining in jail and attempting to expose her husband's corruption.

Helen was all in favor of exposing Franklin's corruption, but the past few days had taught her some hard lessons in the exercise of raw power. She no longer believed that just because Philip was innocent and

Franklin dishonest, then her brother would go free and her husband would face the punishment he deserved. She was quite sure that Franklin had a backup plan already in place that would enable him to shake off any accusations she and Philip could make. In fact, Franklin was more than capable of twisting their accusations into a weapon that would boomerang and destroy both her and her brother.

"For once, Phil, just be thankful that I'm married to a senator, and that Franklin knows some people who could make things happen," she said as they finally walked out of jail, with Philip still hounding her with questions.

Philip frowned. "I'm trying, but I don't understand how he did this. And I hate to sound ungrateful, but I'm having real trouble picturing Franklin going out of his way to help me, of all people. The guy loathes me."

"Well, he did help you," Helen snapped, disliking the lie, but seeing no alternative. Right now, she was focused on getting Philip back to his apartment so that she could persuade him to pack up and leave the state before Franklin found another way to screw him over.

"Sometimes, it's smart not to probe too

deeply into the hows and wherefores," she said, hurrying toward her car, which was parked in a corner of the precinct lot. "Just go with the flow, okay?"

"That doesn't sound like you, Nell. In fact, it's so out of character in terms of advice that it strikes me as real ominous."

"It's not ominous at all. Why can't you accept that Franklin called in a few heavy-duty favors? He persuaded the police to double-check with the witness and Shawn admitted he invented the story of seeing you deal drugs because he wanted to get back at you as vengeance for being dropped from the basketball team."

Philip rolled his eyes in disbelief, and Helen could see why. "Okay, somehow the cops lost their star witness," her brother said. "But there are five hundred grams of coke sitting in the evidence room that still need to be explained away. Why the hell are the police turning me loose just because Shawn backtracked on his story?"

Helen squirmed. There was no way for her to feel comfortable about Franklin's manipulation of the justice system, even though she assumed he had only pulled the same corrupt cop strings to make the drugs vanish as he'd used to get them planted in the first place.

"Why are you looking so damn guilty?" Philip demanded. "Come on, Nell, cough it up."

"Actually . . . um . . . the drugs seem to have disappeared from the evidence room."

"What?" Philip stared at her.

"Be grateful for the bureaucratic screwup. You got lucky."

He snorted in derision. "There's only one way Franklin could have made that coke disappear, and it isn't a lucky screwup. He must have bought off a cop. Or more than one, in fact."

Philip was clearly on the brink of demanding an explanation she wasn't willing to give, and she tried to think of a way to distract him when the sound of a man's voice calling her name provided a welcome diversion. Supremely grateful for the excuse to change the subject, she turned and saw Ryan following them across the parking lot.

A pleasant warmth unfurled in the pit of Helen's stomach as she waited for the detective to catch up with them. Her whole body suddenly felt more alive. Her reaction was crazy, she realized, not to mention inappropriate. Not only was she still a married woman, at least technically, but Ryan had no reason to harbor friendly feelings toward her, given that he believed she'd rejected his proposal simply because a richer and more famous man had come along.

Even with the advantage of hindsight, Helen knew she hadn't been as shallow and grasping as Ryan assumed. In retrospect, though, she realized she'd been misled by her own past experiences. When her mother died of ovarian cancer, her father had gone to pieces, devastated by the loss of the woman he loved. He'd drunk too much, cared too little about his home and kids and taken out his grief in explosions of temper against his fellow workers. He'd been fired from job after job, leaving Helen to worry about paying bills and putting food on the table. Worst of all, in her opinion, her father had used his grief to justify beating up on her younger brother for a long list of imagined sins, when his only true offense had been that he looked too much like their dead mother.

With those experiences in her past, the passion she'd felt for Ryan hadn't struck her as a solid basis for marriage. Her father's behavior convinced her that sexual passion and starry-eyed romance led nowhere good. The fact that Ryan moved through life with such confidence, and found laughter in the simple events of daily life, didn't reassure her. On the contrary, she worried because everything about her relationship with Ryan was way too easy and too much fun. Life wasn't fun, it was deadly serious, at least in her experience.

She worried about what would happen when she and Ryan hit the first real bump in the road. The fact that Ryan was forever advising her to quit cosseting her brother warned her how he would most likely respond. He'd be like her father. At the first hint of real trouble, he'd walk away, at least emotionally, if not physically. If his advice was to walk away from her brother, why would his response to other problems be different?

Franklin Gettys had seemed the antithesis of all that was worrisome about her relationship with Ryan. He certainly didn't take life lightly. In fact, he was downright pompous, but Helen had found his pomposity comforting. Moreover, he was powerful, socially prominent and rich enough to provide the security she craved. Only people who'd never known the fear of facing an empty food cupboard could afford to dismiss the importance of having enough money. She didn't want her marriage to be about love and romance. Her parents had been in love and look what happened to them. She wanted her marriage to be about making a secure home, so the fact that she wasn't sexually attracted to Franklin and that he had no sense of humor didn't bother her in the least.

When you got right down to it, Helen thought with a wry smile, she'd agreed to marry Franklin because absolutely nothing about their relationship had seemed fun or frivolous. In hindsight, those had to be among the least sensible reasons for getting married that she'd ever heard.

Her rueful amusement must have shown on her face. Ryan drew up a couple of feet away from her, his brows drawn together in a ferocious scowl. "I'm glad you find the situation humorous," he said, his teeth visibly clenched.

Why in the world was he looking so angry? "I'm sorry —" Helen pulled herself up short, her pleasure at the unexpected encounter vanishing. Dammit, she was through with apologizing to men when she had no reason to. That destructive pattern had started with her father, been brought to a fine art with her soon-to-be-ex-husband, and wasn't about to continue with Ryan Benton, even if she'd once been in love with him and he was still the best-looking cop she'd ever seen.

She could have ignored him and walked

away. But she was through with avoiding confrontation, too. From now on, the world was going to see a whole new Helen Gettys. Strike that. A whole new Helen Kouros.

She held out the car keys. "Philip, could you go start the car, please? I'll be right with you. Ryan and I need to talk for a moment."

Somewhat to her surprise, her brother took the keys and walked off without comment, leaving her free to respond to Ryan's remark. She tilted her head back so that she could stare straight at him. "Last I heard, there was no law that said citizens aren't allowed to smile. Not even citizens unlucky enough to find themselves at a police station, confronting a pissed-off detective."

"Maybe there should be." Ryan Benton looked as if he meant it. "I'll admit you had me fooled, Helen. Despite your marriage, I had you figured for a woman of integrity who —"

"I am a woman of integrity."

Ryan gave a hard laugh. "Sure you are. That's why you paid somebody to get rid of five hundred grams of coke in the evidence room."

She blushed scarlet. "I . . . didn't pay off anybody." It was a feeble excuse, but how could she explain the truth?

"I'm sure you didn't. Not in person. Why would you get your elegant fingers dirty?"

"You don't know what you're talking about, Ryan, so back the hell off. My brother was set up —"

"Don't!" he said angrily. His voice lowered, and he looked at her with less anger and more sympathy. "You're doing Philip no favors by springing him from jail. Drug addicts have to learn to take responsibility for their actions. How many times did I tell you that already? Trust me on this, Helen, and do your brother a big favor. Let him hit bottom, because that's the essential first step on the road to recovery. He sure as hell won't turn his life around as long as you keep buying him out of trouble."

"You're mighty free with your advice," she said, her feelings raw with accumulated stress. "For your information, Philip is innocent of the charges you're trying to stick him with. He hasn't been near a drug deal in over two years, either as a buyer or a seller. And you can go to hell."

Ryan ran his fingers through his hair, his expression grim. "That seems to be exactly where I'm headed."

"Good. I'm sure you'll fit right in with the other residents." Helen swung on her heel, breathing fast. Her fury was illogical, she knew. She should have been able to show some sympathy for Ryan's frustration. After all, he had been the arresting cop, and from his point of view, Philip's release from jail was a travesty of justice. Money, power and insider contacts had been used to corrupt the judicial system and Ryan had no way of knowing that the system had been corrupted twice, resulting in the release of a man who hadn't deserved to be imprisoned in the first place. Somehow, though, she wasn't willing to empathize with Ryan's frustration. To hell with him, anyway. Why should she care what he thought about her? Their relationship had finished years ago, in another lifetime.

"Not so fast." Ryan grabbed her arm and swung her around again. Helen held his gaze, shaking not only with rage and the traumatic upheavals of the past few days, but also with an emotion she was mortified to identify as sexual desire. It was humiliating to know that her physical attraction to this man remained so powerful.

"Let go of my arm, Detective." Her voice was low-pitched, and throbbing with the intensity of her feelings.

"Or what?" he asked tauntingly.

She sought wildly for an answer. "Or my husband will be forced to demonstrate his displeasure with your behavior."

Ryan looked as if he'd been kicked in the stomach, but he didn't loosen his grip. "Don't threaten me, Helen. Your husband is a dud weapon as far as I'm concerned."

"Are you sure of that, Ryan?"

"I'm one hundred percent sure." Instead of dropping her arm, he almost shoved it against her body. For an endless moment they stared into each other's eyes, generating emotional heat that had very little to do with her brother's release from jail. Then Ryan turned away, striding toward the station house without saying anything more. When Helen realized she was staring with hypnotized fascination at his retreating back, she jerked her gaze away and almost ran the last few yards to her car.

"What was that all about?" Philip asked as she slid behind the wheel. "The pair of you looked as if you were about to come to blows."

She ought to have been grateful that her brother's attention had been temporarily diverted from the disappearance of five hundred grams of coke from the evidence room. Perversely, Helen discovered that she wanted to discuss Ryan Benton even less than she wanted to discuss the true reasons behind her brother's release.

"The detective was annoyed that his case

against you went up in smoke," she said, trying to end the discussion before it began.

"Was he? After the stories I heard during the past twenty-four hours, I assumed he wouldn't care."

Helen frowned, concentrating on easing out of the parking lot into the heavy flow of rush hour traffic. Against her better judgment, she probed her brother's remark. "Why did you think Ryan wouldn't care?"

Philip hesitated for a moment. "I know you used to date him for a while in Silver Rapids —"

"That was over before Franklin and I were married. These days he's barely even an acquaintance."

"That's good. I was afraid you might have bribed him to get me out of jail."

"Bribed *Ryan Benton?*" Helen stopped reversing to stare at her brother.

"Yeah." Her brother paused.

"You know something you're not telling me."

Philip shrugged. "I heard some weird insider stuff from the guy in the cell next to me last night. He's a regular jailhouse inmate and told me there's a huge corruption scandal brewing in the precinct."

Helen was oddly surprised, despite the fact that her brother's arrest was living proof that all was not as it should be with the police department. Still, as big city police departments went, Denver was known for honesty and integrity. "How would some crook in a jail cell know that? I haven't seen a whisper about police corruption on TV or in the newspapers."

"The guy is a street crook," Philip said. "Rap sheet miles long, all for petty offenses. He's currently a runner for one of the drug gangs, and the cops use him as an informant. Every so often, they haul him into jail and leave him there for a couple of nights, just to remind him what could happen if he doesn't cooperate. Anyway, this guy said something about a rumor out on the street that Ryan Benton is about to be brought up on corruption charges as a result of an investigation by Internal Affairs."

"Say that again," Helen ordered, then had to slam on the brakes to prevent the car rolling backward into a bush because she wasn't concentrating. "Ryan Benton has been investigated by the police disciplinary department? He's *officially* suspected of being corrupt?"

"Yeah. At least according to the guy in the next cell." Philip nodded. "Apparently Ryan was involved in an earlier corruption scandal ten years ago, so he's an automatic suspect.

At that time, his partner, Colleen Wellesley, got kicked off the force but he was allowed to resign. I guess they didn't have enough evidence to bring charges or he'd never have been hired as sheriff in Silver Rapids. Or hired back on here in Denver. Kind of surprising, isn't it?"

Incredible, Helen thought. She'd never in a thousand years have figured Ryan Benton for a bought cop. The possibility that he might be in Franklin's pay hadn't once crossed her mind, even though he'd been the arresting officer on Philip's case, and even though she knew that Franklin had to be bribing somebody in the precinct. She drew in a deep breath, fighting a sudden wave of nausea.

"What exactly is Ryan accused of doing?" she asked. "Did your informant explain?"

"He's not been formally accused of anything so far, but apparently he and his partner are both accused of taking bribes to look the other way at crime scenes. Guess he fooled me, even though he was the one who busted me on a phony charge." Philip shook his head. "Ryan looks an honest, down-to-earth kind of guy. To be truthful, I kinda liked him. Insofar as you can like a cop who's busting your ass."

"It just shows how looks can be deceiving." Helen managed to sound casual enough, but the nausea wouldn't go away. Her stomach was churning with so much acid that she thought she might actually throw up.

"You didn't get any hint he was dirty when you were dating him?" Philip asked.

"Not a thing, or our dating days would have been over." At least she could answer that honestly. "I never heard or saw anything to suggest he was dishonest. He was the town sheriff, you know, and his reputation in Silver Rapids was just about golden."

"Maybe the big city got to him."

"Maybe."

The lying hypocrite, Helen thought, putting all the facts about Ryan Benton together and coming up with a new and unpleasant picture. The mealy-mouthed bastard had dared to complain to her about Philip's release from jail when all the time he was part of the very corruption he appeared to condemn. Her conversation with him took on a different significance once she considered the likelihood that Ryan was dirty, and his parting remark suddenly struck her in a whole new light.

Your husband is a dud weapon. Helen had taken that to mean that Ryan was an honest cop who refused to be intimidated by the power of Senator Franklin Gettys. But if Ryan was already in Franklin's pay, his remark might mean simply that he had nothing to fear. In fact, she reflected grimly, Ryan and Franklin could well be allies. The idea made sense. Ryan had made the bust, so nothing could have been easier than for him to cook up the case against Philip in the first place.

Seething with outrage, Helen added up the indictment against Ryan. Franklin had been talking to him at the cocktail party the other night. Why else would her husband waste his time with a lowly detective from one of the city's less affluent neighborhoods unless the guy was in his pocket? Add to that the fact that Ryan had been the arresting cop when her brother was set up on a fake charge, orchestrated by her husband, and it began to seem more and more likely that Ryan had been paid off to do Franklin's bidding.

Helen felt a disappointment that was painful, even if irrational. Until a few days ago, she and Ryan hadn't spoken to each other in two and a half years, so there was no reason for her to feel as if she'd been personally betrayed. Still, it was yet another lesson learned in a week that was already too full of difficult lessons. How many times did she need to have it hammered home that you couldn't judge the heart of a man from his handsome exterior?

"You okay, Nell?" Philip touched her lightly on the arm.

"Yes, sure. I'm fine now you're out of jail." With considerable effort, she dragged her attention away from Ryan Benton and back to her brother. Right now, all that mattered was that she should get her brother out of state, far away from Franklin and his corrupt cronies. And then, as soon as Philip was safely out of reach, Helen could fight for her own freedom from a marriage that had turned into the worst sort of prison.

She was counting not just the weeks or the days, but the hours and the minutes.

Chapter Eight

Seattle, September, 16 months later
Labour Day was barely past, but Seattle had already given up on summer sunshine. Helen shivered as the drizzling rain trickled under her umbrella and soaked through her linen jacket. Her clunker of a car was in the shop — again — so she'd been forced to take the bus to and from her work at Nordstrom's flagship department store.

She was cold and soaked through, but Helen didn't mind the discomfort. She was human enough to heave an occasional nostalgic sigh for the BMW sports coupe that had vanished along with her marriage, but taking the bus every so often seemed a small price to pay for the glorious gift of freedom from Franklin Gettys. She hadn't realized how desperately unhappy she'd been in her marriage until it had ended and she had headed west to join her brother in Seattle.

Her idle days in the lonely Cherry Hills

mansion were a fast-fading memory that brought only relief, not regrets. Nowadays, she lived in a rented row house and worked long hours for modest pay. An outsider might think that her life had taken a sharp turn for the worse. Helen knew it had taken a fantastic turn for the better.

She sidestepped a puddle, missed, and was rewarded with water sloshing inside her shoes. Her life might be better in a general sense, she reflected with an inward smile, but right at this moment she was looking forward to getting home and enjoying a hot bath, scented with something luxuriously seductive. That is, if bath oil bought at a discount drugstore could be considered luxurious. Helen grinned. At least she'd bought the cheap pink stuff herself, and that made the perfume incredibly sweet.

Her steps and her thoughts both slammed to an abrupt halt as a trench-coated woman blocked the sidewalk in front of her. The woman was holding a mike, which she thrust out under Helen's nose.

"I'm Desiree Shelton from Eyewitness News," she said. "You are Helen Gettys, the former wife of Senator Franklin Gettys, right?"

"I have no comment about anything,"

Helen said. Belatedly — very belatedly — she realized there were half a dozen people clustered outside the modest row house that she and Philip rented. There was also a minivan with the logo of a local TV station parked right across from their rickety front gate.

What the hell had Franklin said or done now, Helen wondered wearily. She was so tired of her ex-husband's seemingly endless need to make her the butt of stories leaked to the media, designed to show her as an adulterous alcoholic, and himself as the wonderful man who'd struggled to bring her to salvation, failing only because of Helen's willful refusal to accept his loving help.

Whatever story he'd concocted this time, she wouldn't dignify it with a denial. If there was one thing she'd learned in the months following her divorce, it was that there was absolutely nothing she could say to the media that would cause them to slant their stories in any way other than the direction they'd always intended — usually negative to her and praising Franklin to the skies.

"Excuse me, please." She tried to pass the Eyewitness News reporter. "It's been a long day at work and I'd like to get inside my own home. You're blocking my entrance."

"Would you care to comment on the kidnapping case of baby Sky Langworthy, Mrs. Gettys?"

Helen reared back and stared directly into the reporter's eyes. "Why on earth are you asking me about the Langworthy kidnapping?" she asked, startled out of her standard no-comment response.

"You haven't heard about the statement your brother made earlier this morning?"

Helen shook her head in bemusement. Was it possible that Philip had commented on the kidnapping of the three-month-old baby grandson of a former governor of Colorado? That seemed not just incredible, but bizarre. Why would her brother make a statement? And who would care if he did?

Young man who has no insider information, knows none of the parties involved, and lives a thousand miles away from the scene of the kidnapping, makes public statement about the Schyler Langworthy kidnapping.

Yep, she could sure see how that would bring all the press hounds salivating.

Helen was media-savvy enough not to utter a single word of what she was thinking. "I haven't heard anything about any statement my brother might have made," she said, hoping that she sounded calmer than she felt. "We've never discussed the kidnapping. Excuse me, please. I have no comment to make at this time."

"But you'll have a statement to make later, Mrs. Gettys?" the reporter asked eagerly.

Helen shook her head. "I have nothing to say now, or at any time in the future. Oh, and by the way, my name is Helen Kouros. I'm sure you are aware that Senator Gettys and I are no longer married."

She dodged around Desiree What'sHer-Name and sprinted up the path to the front door. Thank goodness Philip must have been watching from inside the house, because he tugged open the door before she had even started looking for her key, and dragged her inside.

Helen slumped against the inside of the door, umbrella dripping onto the worn linoleum floor. The house had been built in the nineteen forties, when Seattle was practically a frontier town, and had a minuscule entrance hall with doors that opened to a tiny parlor on one side and an even smaller dining room on the other. Right now, she was glad the hallway had no windows. It was good to be shielded from prying eyes, and she felt pleasantly cocooned in the enclosed space, a comforting contrast to the harassment waiting on the outside of the door.

"What in the world was that about?" she demanded, too stressed even to take the necessary few steps into the parlor. "Why do we have a TV crew camped out on our doorstep?"

"Haven't you heard?" Philip's smile was bitter. "I'm the media's latest hot suspect in the kidnapping of the Langworthy baby."

Helen almost laughed. Almost. "Why in the world would anyone suspect you of kidnapping the Langworthy baby?" Helen was glad she had the front door to hold her upright. "Are they nuts? Quite apart from anything else, you're here in Seattle and the baby was kidnapped from his crib in Denver —"

"Yeah, you're right. Unfortunately, the baby was snatched on the Fourth of July —"

"And so?"

"That's when I was camping in the Colorado Rockies."

"Oh no! Oh damn!"

"Oh yes," Philip said bleakly. "I was gone for a week, remember?"

"But you were camping with friends! They can provide an alibi for you."

Philip shook his head. "I was only with friends for the first five days. On the Fourth, the campground was swarming with tourists, so the other guys went home a day early and I hiked way up into the mountains and slept out for the night."

There was no way her brother could have guessed what a rotten idea that would turn out to be. Helen damped down her frustration. "Okay, but you weren't alone all the time, were you? Somebody must have seen you."

"Yeah, I guess people saw me," Philip said, sounding gloomy. "But it's more than three months later. I bet there's not a chance of finding a witness who could swear they saw me in the Arapahoe National Forest at the time Schyler was taken from his crib. The reporters have it all worked out, it seems. They claim I had enough time to hike down out of the forest, drive into Denver and snatch the baby."

"Then they're nuts! You were miles away from Denver."

"I had a rental car, remember, so it's physically possible I could have done the deed, although even the FBI agrees I must have had an accomplice helping me because I didn't have any baby with me later that evening when I met up with another friend for dinner."

"The FBI?" Helen said, her voice sharpening with worry. "Don't tell me that law enforcement is paying attention to this latest load of media garbage?"

"They're paying enough attention for two agents to come out to the college campus this afternoon and question me for three hours. Although they didn't hold me when I kept saying I knew nothing at all about the kidnapping. I guess that's one minor blessing."

"And who does the FBI believe is your accomplice?" Helen asked, although she was afraid she already knew the answer to that question.

"Well, since Franklin Gettys is undoubtedly the bastard who leaked this bullshit to the media, I'll give you one guess about who they suspect."

She swallowed. "Me?"

"Bingo. Give the lady a prize. That son of a bitch you were married to has stuck it to us again."

"Oh my God." A wave of pessimism washed over Helen, even though she knew the media interest in her couldn't hold up. She'd been at a barbecue on the Fourth right here in Seattle, and she could prove it. But the prospect of fighting off the press again really depressed her. She should have known the past ten months living in Seattle had been much too peaceful after the tumultuous period of her divorce from Franklin Gettys.

Sighing, she pushed her hair out of her eyes. She couldn't afford fancy haircuts anymore, and she'd let it grow long so that she could wear it swept back into a chignon — the cheapest of all styles.

"Let me get out of these damp clothes," she said to her brother, needing a few minutes to grasp the full implications of what he'd told her. "Then we'll have a family conference and decide how we're going to handle this —"

"Actually, we have a visitor."

"Cathie's here?" Helen said, her mood perking up a little. Philip had been dating seriously for the past five months, and Helen thought that in Cathie, a nurse with a graduate degree in obstetrics, her brother might have found the perfect future wife. Not to mention a sister Helen would love to have.

Philip shook his head. "Not Cathie, although I'm going over to her apartment later tonight. Ryan Benton's come from Colorado to see us. He's waiting in the parlor."

Ryan Benton was here, in her house? Helen forgot all about changing out of her damp clothes. She pushed open the door and marched into the parlor, where Ryan Benton was indeed waiting. He rose to his feet, looking tall and dominating in the tiny room. He also looked spectacularly handsome, but she did her best not to notice that annoying fact. In her opinion, one of the few things more despicable than a crooked politician was a dirty cop, and she had no intention of allowing her physical attraction to Ryan Benton to override her ethical standards.

"What are you doing here?" she demanded.

Ryan gave an infuriatingly controlled smile, his gaze traveling slowly upward from her mud-splattered shoes, past her damp jacket and skirt, and coming to rest on her disheveled hair. "It's nice to see you, too, Helen."

By the time he'd finished his inspection, she felt as elegant and put-together as something the cat had dragged out onto the back stoop to finish eating. She pushed a strand of damp hair behind her ear, ignoring the drips onto her neck. She drew herself up to her full height, which meant that she was still seven inches shorter than Ryan's six foot two, and glared up at him.

"I assume you have a reason for being here. Please state it and then leave."

"I'm investigating the kidnapping of Schyler Langworthy —"

"Then you're in the wrong place, because Philip and I know nothing about the kidnapping. Goodbye."

"I think you can help me with my investigation —"

"I know you're not a cop anymore, Ryan, so how can you be investigating a kidnapping?" Helen didn't want to listen to him lie, so she told him what she knew. "I heard all about the corruption charges made against you and your partner. I know you both left the police department under a very large black cloud. There were lengthy reports about you and your partner in the Denver newspapers at least two months before I moved from Colorado to Seattle."

If anything, Ryan's expression became more bland. "The newspapers didn't give an entirely accurate account of what happened. Despite the lurid reporting, my partner and I were never formally accused of anything. The truth is, we chose to resign."

"In other words, you made your escape one step ahead of the law." Helen had been a victim of distorted media reporting often enough that she ought to have been willing to give Ryan and his partner the benefit of the doubt. But for once everything she knew personally backed up the published reports. She knew for a fact that Ryan had been bribed by Franklin Gettys to frame Philip for drug dealing. She would never forgive him for that injury to her brother.

Her caustic comment caused the faintest tightening of Ryan's mouth. Maybe he wasn't quite as indifferent to her barbs as his neutral expression might suggest. Helen was obscurely pleased to know that she had the power to get under his skin, even if only marginally.

"Are you planning for us to spend the next few minutes trading insults?" Ryan asked. "If so, I can give back as good as I get. Or should we simply take the insults as a given and move on to the real reason why I'm here?"

"We should move on," she said tightly. But there was a definite appeal to the idea of trading insults. Her skin felt prickly with irritation at Ryan's presence here in her new home. She was tired of the way he kept popping back into her life, disturbing her equilibrium. Most of all, she despised the way her body reacted to his physical attractions, despite what she knew about his moral worth. Or lack thereof. Apparently marriage to Franklin Gettys hadn't rammed home the elementary lesson that good looks had nothing to do with character.

"Okay, then. We'll skip the insults." Ryan was definitely losing some of his cool. He drew in a sharp breath and spoke with visibly hard-won calm. "As I started to explain, I'm helping to investigate the disappearance of Schyler Langworthy. A member of the baby's immediate family has hired my company to help find him."

"Hired your company?" Helen asked. "Do you work for a firm of private investigators, then?"

Ryan nodded. "Yes, I do. When I was sheriff of Silver Rapids, I worked on a case with a woman called Colleen Wellesley. She started her own investigative agency some years back, and she invited me to come and work for her at Investigations, Confidential and Undercover. She needed the extra help." He gave a tight smile. "Investigating sleazy activities seems to be a recession-proof business."

"Yes, there's always plenty of sleazy activity to go around, isn't there?" Helen said sweetly. She was surprised Ryan and Colleen Wellesley had managed to get their detective company licensed. Or perhaps she wasn't. After all, they had corrupt friends in high places. No doubt Franklin Gettys and his cronies found it useful to keep gofers who had their fingers on the pulse of Denver's criminal underbelly. If Franklin couldn't have Ryan operating from inside the heart of the police force, having him on tap as a private investigator was probably the next best thing.

"That still doesn't explain what you're doing here in my house," she said. "If you believe my brother and I have anything to do with Schyler's disappearance, I can only tell you one more time that you're entirely mistaken."

Ryan looked unimpressed by her vehemence. "Mistaken or not, you're both going to face a lot of questions. Channel 12 broke the story of Philip's possible involvement yesterday afternoon. I followed up with the FBI, expecting them to tell me I should pay no attention. Instead, the FBI agent in charge of the case confirmed that Philip was 'a person of interest' to the investigation. Given our firm's involvement in the case, I had no choice but to come out here and investigate why the bureau believes your brother can help them with their inquiries."

Helen smothered a flare of anger at the FBI agent who could so casually toss her brother to the wolves. "The bureau has a bad habit of identifying 'persons of interest' who later turn out to have nothing at all to do with the case they're investigating. If the bureau truly believes Philip is involved in the kidnapping of Schyler Langworthy, then they're dead wrong. I'm sorry for the Langworthy family and what they're suffering, but we can't help them. In fact, I can't imagine why my brother let you into our home. We have nothing to say to you or to the FBI, and I'd appreciate it if you'd leave."

Helen jumped to her feet and pointedly held the parlor door open. She wanted Ryan out of her sight before she started to recall too much about the happy times they'd shared in Silver Rapids during the nine months they'd dated. In her memories, the days unfolded as a fun-filled G-rated movie, accompanied by a soundtrack filled with laughter, music, and lighthearted conversation. The nights blurred into a triple X-rated movie with a soundtrack of heavy breathing and low moans of sexual pleasure.

Helen blinked, hurriedly returning her attention to the present. If she carried on with that train of thought much longer, her damp clothes would soon be steaming.

"Goodbye, Ryan," she said, with a firmness that was as much for herself as for him. "Have a safe flight home to Colorado."

"Not so fast," he said, not moving. "Let me remind you I'm in this house at your brother's specific invitation."

"Then I can only assume some alien has swooped down and taken possession of his body because my real brother would never invite you into our home." Helen remained by the door, fingers tapping on the handle.

"Well, here he comes. Ask him yourself." Ryan gestured toward Philip, who was entering the parlor at that moment, carrying a tray with three steaming mugs of coffee mixed with hot milk — his homemade version of café latte. Three mugs, Helen noted. It seemed Ryan was correct in claiming that her brother had invited him to stay for a while. What's more, her brother looked positively friendly as he came into the parlor and aimed a smile in Ryan's direction.

Possession by space aliens began to look more and more likely. How else to explain Philip's amiability? After her divorce, she'd told her brother the truth about the drug charges that had been brought against him, including the fact that Ryan was the cop who'd helped Franklin to set him up. Not surprisingly, her brother had been outraged. If Ryan hadn't already been dismissed from the force, her brother would have launched a one-man crusade to get him convicted of corruption. And now here Philip was, suddenly all smiles toward the man he'd sworn vengeance against less than nine months ago.

"How far did Ryan get in telling you what's going on?" Philip asked, handing his sister a mug of coffee. "Here Ryan. You don't take sugar, right? Did you already explain to Nell why you're here?"

"We barely got started," Ryan said smoothly, taking his coffee with a murmur of thanks. "Your sister and I were still catching up on a few personal details."

Philip dropped into his favorite chair, draping his long legs over the arm. That left Helen nowhere to sit except on the sofa, next to Ryan. Spine ramrod straight, she perched as far away from him as space allowed, wrapping her hands around the warm mug. Just because her brother had taken leave of his senses, there was no need for her to do the same. She'd listen to Ryan's excuses for being here and then she'd show him the door.

For some reason better left unexamined, the prospect of his departure didn't make her as happy as it should have.

Chapter Nine

Far from showing animosity toward the man who'd arrested him, Philip seemed entirely relaxed and friendly as he sipped his coffee. "We'd better fill Helen in on the details of the Langworthy baby's disappearance," he said to Ryan. He smiled affectionately toward his sister. "She's such a softie that she hasn't been following the case very closely. She says it's too painful to imagine what the baby's family is going through, so she prefers to avoid hearing the details. That way, her imagination can't go into overdrive."

"Then here's a really condensed version of what happened," Ryan said, turning on the sofa to face Helen. "Schyler Langworthy was kidnapped from his crib on the morning of July 4. He was three months old at the time. His mother is Holly Langworthy, and she's a single parent —"

Helen nodded. "And I remember that Holly's father is Samuel Langworthy, who was the governor of Colorado most of the time I was in grade school."

"And now Holly's half brother, Joshua, is running for governor in the upcoming election," Ryan said. "Governor Forbes, the incumbent, went into the election campaign with quite a few negatives to overcome, but he's proving a surprisingly difficult opponent to beat."

"He's a good campaigner," Helen conceded. "I met the governor on a couple of occasions when I was married to Franklin, and he's a tough old bird." She hadn't been very impressed with Todd Forbes, she reflected, who had seemed big on charm and short on genuine warmth — a similar personality to Franklin, in fact. She knew from TV and newspaper commentaries that her ex and Governor Forbes were political allies who shared an enthusiasm for bio-weapons research that they both tried to pass off as nothing more than a desire to bring high-tech jobs to Colorado. Given their personalities, Helen suspected that job creation was low on their list of priorities. What they both wanted was the power that would come from controlling a new weapons program.

"As you can imagine, there are a lot of high-powered people desperate for Schyler to be found," Ryan said, sipping his coffee.

"The baby's disappearance is not just a tragedy for the Langworthys. It's giving the local cops a severe attack of heartburn, and creating a ton of unfavorable publicity for the FBI. The press commentary has gotten so scathing that the FBI director sent an official letter of rebuke to the Denver FBI office. As you can imagine, they're not happy about that, to put it mildly."

Much as Helen disliked thinking along such lines, the absence of progress in the case seemed to suggest that baby Schyler might already be dead. She shuddered in sympathy for what Holly Langworthy was going through. She couldn't imagine a worse nightmare than having your baby snatched from his crib, followed by months of silence about his fate.

"From what little I know about the case, the public's been very supportive," she said, trying not to dwell on the disturbing image of Holly's grief. "Aren't the police getting any tips on their hotline?"

"There have been plenty of tips," Ryan said. "But they've all petered out, and right now the agent in charge admitted to me that the case is on a high-speed track to nowhere."

Philip folded a paper napkin to make a coaster for his coffee mug. "Meanwhile, the cable TV channels are blanketing the airwaves with around-the-clock coverage, so every kook with an ax to grind can find an outlet to get publicity for his nutty theory. Naming me as a suspect is just the latest flaky theory in a long line of them."

"And the rival political camps in the governor's race aren't helping," Ryan said. "The two camps are hurling accusations at each other, each one claiming that the other guys are trying to make election capital out of the baby's disappearance."

Helen felt another wave of sympathy for Holly Langworthy, who was coping not only with the devastating disappearance of her son, but also with media speculation that was downright vicious. "I *despise* the way politicians manage to make even a tragedy like the kidnapping of a baby into campaign propaganda," she said.

"Yeah, it's been depressing to watch," Ryan said. "Especially since Josh Langworthy has some interesting new ideas to put to the electorate. It's a shame he's not getting a chance to campaign on the issues, instead of constantly being asked about his missing nephew. However, you two can't afford to spare any sympathy for other people. Right now, you need to look out for yourselves because unless you act fast, you're going to be dragged front and center of the media circus —"

"I don't see how," Helen said. "Surely to goodness this interest in Philip is going to be a one-day wonder on the cable news channels and then all the speculation in us will die down again."

Ryan shook his head. "You're not going to escape that easily. My contact at the bureau told me their sudden interest in your brother wasn't just fueled by media hunger for new suspects. It seems the bureau received an anonymous package that contained detailed information outlining how and why Philip was involved in kidnapping Schyler Langworthy."

"That must have been a slender package," Helen said tartly.

"The evidence is circumstantial but it fits convincingly together," Philip said, scowling into his empty coffee mug. "They even have a motive as to why I might have done it. They claim I have a crazy, drug-induced desire to get back at Holly Langworthy."

"But you don't even know Holly Langworthy!" Helen exclaimed.

"I do know her a little," Philip admitted. "Or at least I did. I dated her years ago, but for less than a month — it was when you were working at the Swansong Casino, Nell, so you weren't often in Denver, which is why you didn't know about it."

"You're right, I had no idea you'd ever set eyes on her, much less dated her," Helen said. "Is the FBI correct? Did she dump you?"

"Yep, she dumped me all right," Philip said wryly. "I was heavily into cocaine at the time, so I don't remember all the details of our traumatic parting scene, but I know it was related to my drug use and I'm sure I deserved whatever insults she heaped on my spaced-out head. As for wanting to get back at her . . . well, that's nuts. To be honest, I hadn't thought about Holly from the day we split up until the day I heard Schyler had been kidnapped. The fact is, I never really knew much about her, except that she was real pretty and a cool date to take to a party."

"Did you explain all this to the FBI?" Helen asked.

"Yeah, but straight-arrow FBI agents aren't the types to have much personal experience with the highs and lows of drug addiction. It's hard for them to grasp how superficial my relationships were back then, and how little connection I feel nowadays to that part of my past. They think I'm holding back information, when really I don't have any to give them."

Helen counted off on her fingers. "Okay, so you have no alibi, the media is pursuing us and the FBI seems to be considering both of us as possible suspects —"

"The FBI aren't going to arrest Philip, much less you," Ryan said. "As soon as they run a serious investigation of the accusations, they'll realize they don't have a case."

"Great," Helen said. "So we won't get arrested, we'll just get convicted by the media. Are we going to sit around and wait for our lives to be destroyed before we get serious about demonstrating that these crazy theories have no basis except in my ex-husband's desire for vengeance?" Instinctively, she turned to Ryan as she spoke.

"Are you asking me?" he said quietly.

She hesitated for a moment, realizing the incongruity of looking for help from a man she had no reason to trust. "I guess I am," she said finally. "You're the detective, after all."

"I'm a detective you accused of being corrupt only a few minutes ago."

Helen pushed at the loose strands of her hair again, as if taming her hairstyle would somehow enable her to make sense out of her muddled thoughts. Ryan leaned toward her and caught her hand, keeping it in his clasp.

"Let's face facts, Helen, even if they're uncomfortable. We can't work together unless the two of us get some personal issues out on the table."

"What sort of personal issues?" Helen asked, instantly wary.

"At a minimum, issues about honesty and integrity," Ryan said. "Not just mine, but yours, too. I came here believing I had good reasons to distrust you and your brother. Ever since Philip escaped so easily from that drug dealing charge, I've blamed you. I convinced myself you were so overprotective where he was concerned that you'd lost your judgment. I believed you were willing to use your influence with Franklin Gettys to corrupt the system and get the drug charges against your brother thrown out —"

"Well, you were right," she said. "I did exactly that, but for a valid reason. The charges against Philip were false." Confusion made her voice harsh. "You of all people should know that."

"I know it *now*," Ryan said. "That's because Philip spent the two hours before you arrived home from work filling me in on the details of how Franklin blackmailed you into staying with him. But I had no idea your brother had been set up when I arrested him last spring. At the time I didn't have a clue what was going on, I swear it. I was a victim of Franklin Gettys every bit as much as you and Philip."

Ryan sounded so honest, so sincere. So goddamn *trustworthy*. Helen jerked her hand out of his grasp, curling it into a fist because it required real physical effort not to touch him, not to give in to the temptation of taking him at his word. She so much wanted to believe that he could be trusted. Out of the blue, the thought sprang into her mind that Ryan might have been sent here on Franklin's orders, with instructions to worm his way back into her confidence. Her stomach heaved in revulsion at the thought.

"You may have convinced my brother that you didn't know the score when you arrested him, but I have the best of reasons for believing that you were a dirty cop," she said. "I didn't just pull the accusations out of thin air. I know my husband was paying you off." Her voice lowered as she admitted the truth. "I wish I didn't."

She wasn't angry anymore, Helen realized, simply sad. When she was with Ryan, it was so hard to believe that he was one of the bad guys.

"The accusations against my partner were false," Ryan said tersely. "And even the department didn't attempt to bring corruption charges against me. They knew they'd be laughed out of court. As for the accusation that your husband was paying me off . . . what evidence do you have for suggesting that?"

"The best. Before our divorce was finalized, Franklin flat out admitted to me that you were in his pay, and that you were the cop he'd bribed in order to get Philip arrested. In other words, I have proof right from the horse's mouth."

"And you believe Franklin's accusations?" Ryan asked, his voice harsh. "Knowing me as well as you once did, you still believe your ex-husband's words over mine? Did it never occur to you that Franklin might have reasons to lie about which cop he was paying off?"

"Why would he lie about something like that? What advantage would there be to him in that?" But even as Helen asked the question, she realized the answer.

Ryan shot her an incredulous glance. "Why would Franklin Gettys make a false accusation against me?" He laughed without mirth. "Gee, off the top of my head, I can't come up with more than a half dozen reasons. Here's one. He accused me because he was protecting somebody else on the police force. Somebody who was in a much more powerful position than me, and much more useful to him."

"With all the hundreds of cops in Denver, why did Franklin just happen to pick on you to accuse?"

Ryan shrugged as if the answer to her question were obvious. "Partly because he found out you and I had once been lovers and I'm sure it gave him a lot of satisfaction to get me in trouble. I don't think you ever realized just how jealous Franklin was of you, and especially of the popularity you'd achieved in the Silver Rapids community. But there was an even more important reason. I had begun to suspect who the dirty cops might really be and I was working to collect evidence to present to Internal Affairs. Not to mince words, Josie and I were beginning to scare the shit out of your ex-husband."

"Which cops do you suspect of being dirty?" Helen asked.

Ryan shook his head. "We have no proof that would stand up in court and I'm not willing to make accusations that I can't back up. There's been way too much of that happening recently."

"So I'm just supposed to take your word that you never accepted a bribe?"

"Yes, you are." Ryan leaned toward her,

reaching for her hands again and folding them into his. "I'm asking you to trust me, Nell. Is that so impossible?"

When he used that gentle, coaxing voice, he could probably have convinced her that Santa Claus was going to be late delivering toys this year because of an industrial dispute with his elves.

His thumbs stroked across her knuckles. "Before Philip's arrest, however messed up our relationship was, you never had any reason to doubt my integrity, right? So the major reason you suspect me of being corrupt is because of your ex-husband's accusations, right?"

She nodded.

"Consider everything you know about Franklin and everything you know about me. Think about it, Nell. Who is more likely to be telling you the truth?"

Only two people in the world ever called her Nell. One was her brother, and the other was Ryan. Helen's resistance melted some more under the heat of remembered passion. She stared at Ryan's strong, lean hands wrapped around hers and wondered how in the world she was supposed to make rational judgments when all she wanted to do was lay her head against his shoulder and count the world well lost for love.

Getting honest cops thrown off the police force in order to divert suspicion from the real culprits fit the pattern of everything Franklin had done since the day she'd asked for a divorce, Helen reflected. But was that an objective assessment or an expression of her own prejudices? The temptation to believe in Ryan was so strong that she was afraid to give in to it, and she forced herself to make one more protest.

"You have no way to prove that you weren't being paid off by Franklin Gettys," she pointed out.

"No, I don't, but how does anybody prove a negative? It can't be done." Ignoring the fact that Philip was still in the parlor and was watching them with considerable interest, Ryan crooked his finger under her chin and tilted her face up so that she was looking straight into his eyes.

"Sometimes you have to trust your instincts, Nell, and that's always been tough for you. I can't shake the accusation that I'm corrupt without bringing the real dirty cops to justice, and so far we haven't managed to find the evidence for that. It's difficult working from outside the force, especially since the suspects I'm targeting hold such senior positions. But you're in the same situation as me, aren't you? You have no proof that Franklin orchestrated your brother's arrest on drug charges, and no way to prove that he's deliberately making false accusations about the Langworthy kidnapping, so the two of you are stuck under a cloud of suspicion, with no way to dispel the media attention. It's a mess, but unless you and I find some way to trust each other, Franklin Gettys will win."

"Even if we decide to trust each other, Franklin remains more powerful than either of us."

"Don't be so sure of that. I have some powerful friends myself." Ryan touched her lightly on her cheek. "Don't let him win, Nell. Trust me, not him. For once in your life, listen to you heart, not your head."

She'd listened to her head when she rejected Ryan's proposal. She'd listened to it again when she'd agreed to marry Franklin. Ruefully, Helen acknowledged that her head had made bad mistakes on both occasions. Why not trust her feelings for once? The screwup that might result surely couldn't be any worse than what had already happened.

She let out a long, unsteady breath and took a flying leap into unknown territory. "I do trust you, Ryan."

"Wise woman," he said softly. "Smart decision."

Helen only realized how hard it had been to cling to her suspicions about him when she felt her entire body go limp with relief. After almost eighteen months of telling herself that Ryan Benton was as crooked as they come, it should have been difficult to transform her mental images of him from dirty cop to just another victim of Franklin's machinations. Instead, it was one of the easiest things she'd ever done. Despite all the apparent evidence, she'd never managed to fit Ryan into the role of corrupt cop because it went against the grain of everything she knew about him. Franklin in the role of liar and manipulator, on the other hand, was a smooth and easy fit.

"I just wish that trusting each other made a real difference to Franklin's power to create mischief," she said.

"It makes all the difference in the world to me," Ryan said simply.

"It doesn't bring you any closer to finding Schyler Langworthy."

"With your help, I may even have an idea or two about that. We need to pool our information and see if that doesn't give us a new and better perspective. To be honest, what puzzles me most right now is why

Franklin is wasting so much time and energy on blackening your reputation. I never had the impression that Franklin was deeply in love with you, but was I wrong? Is he so brokenhearted that he isn't able to be rational?"

"Franklin's heart never played any role in our marriage," Helen said. "He married me for political convenience, that's all."

"That answer just raises more questions. Why did Franklin find you such a convenient wife? If it's convenience he wanted, wouldn't he have done better to marry a woman who was already active in politics? Or at least a wife who could bring him lots of money to help out with his campaigns?"

"On the surface, you might think so. But Franklin only looked around for a wife because he had to, not because he wanted to. His fortieth birthday was long gone and he was getting too old to remain single —"

"Too old to be single?" Ryan queried. "You mean because he campaigns as a conservative, with a big emphasis on traditional family values?"

She nodded. "Exactly. His core constituents are suspicious of middle-aged bachelors, so he needed to marry. But from Franklin's point of view, that need was a real pain. To be fair, he works hard, for long hours, and his schedule is erratic, making it difficult to coordinate his comings and goings with another person. Plus, he likes living alone. He enjoys eating all his meals in restaurants and going out every night with business colleagues. He also likes having sex with lots of young women he barely knows, and he doesn't want children. How does a wife fit into this picture?"

"Not easily," Ryan said.

"Not at all, in fact." Helen picked up her mug, realized the coffee was all gone, and set it down with a thump, still angry with herself for having been such an easy dupe. "Franklin never planned to be sexually faithful, and he didn't intend to let his wife share the political limelight. Even the need to please the voters wasn't enough to persuade him to have children, or change his lifestyle in any significant way. So he married me, the next best thing to having no wife at all. He figured he had me captive since I had no money, no high-powered friends and no dazzling career to fall back on if I got tired of being a doormat."

"Not to mention your pain-in-the-ass younger brother who had a problem with cocaine," Philip interjected. "I wouldn't be surprised if Franklin saw blackmail opportunities in my addiction problems right from the start. I'll bet he always saw your love for me as something that could be exploited to keep you in line if you ever got too independent."

"What a fool Franklin Gettys was," Ryan said softly.

"Yes, he is. As far as he's concerned, love is a weakness." Helen stared blindly at the hearth but, for a moment, what she saw wasn't the cozy parlor, but the formal living room of Franklin's house in Cherry Hills, where the two of them had shared no more than a dozen evenings in two years of marriage. She shivered at the bleak memory.

"I understand why Franklin married you and why he didn't want you to divorce him," Ryan said. "But I still don't understand why he's going after you now that the marriage is over. Why does he spend so much time blackening your reputation with the media?"

"His assessment of me has changed," Helen suggested. "I think . . . maybe . . . he's a little afraid of me and he wants to make sure the threat I present is neutralized."

"What threat do you represent?" Ryan demanded. "You said yourself that he's the person with all the power."

"Most of the power, not all, otherwise we'd still be married," Helen corrected.

"Once Philip was safe here in Seattle, I began looking for a blackmail weapon to use against Franklin. I decided I needed information — something damaging that I could threaten him with. I knew he'd only agree to a divorce if it was more trouble to keep me in the marriage than to let me go —"

"I suggested she should collect a file with the names of all the women who'd had affairs with him and take it to the media," Philip said.

"But I decided that wasn't fair to the women," Helen said.

"Hell, you're more generous than I would have been," Ryan said. "They were women who'd been committing adultery with your husband —"

"Yes, but I'm sure he told them I was a total bitch who made his life hell, so they have some excuse."

"Not much of a one," Ryan said.

"Maybe not. But more to the point, the fact that Franklin had been unfaithful didn't strike me as formidable enough to be a real weapon. Even his conservative friends might have forgiven him a few episodes of adultery, given the unflattering picture he's managed to paint of me. An alcoholic wife who refuses to sleep with her husband or to share in his political career doesn't generate much sympathy."

"So what did you find to use against him, if not his adultery?" Ryan asked.

"I found the Half Spur," Helen said. "It's a ranch near Granby, where Franklin runs two thousand head of Merino sheep —"

"I'm very familiar with the Half Spur," Ryan said. "The ranch attracted the attention of my partners months ago. We even have a scrap of evidence from the ranch that possibly links Franklin as a suspect in the Langworthy kidnapping."

Helen looked up quickly. "Could Sky be at the ranch, do you think? It's a pretty big place, with lots of convenient trailers and huts where you could hide a baby."

Ryan shook his head. "We had the same idea, but there's no evidence we can find that Sky's ever been taken to the ranch, much less held there."

Helen gave a half nod. "On second thought, I can't imagine that Franklin would take the risk of hiding the baby at the Half Spur, even if he is involved in the kidnapping. He's absolutely paranoid about keeping outsiders away from there."

"I notice that you don't seem shocked by the idea that Franklin might be a kidnapper."

Helen was silent for a moment, realizing how horrifying it was that she'd accepted the idea of her ex-husband as a brutal kidnapper without a murmur of protest. "No, I guess I'm not surprised or shocked," she said finally. "It seems perfectly credible to me that Franklin would kidnap a child if it suited his purpose. And if he thought he could get away with it, of course."

Ryan leaned toward her, so focused that Helen felt the intensity of his concentration as a physical presence. "You had the inside track where Franklin Gettys is concerned, Nell, and that means you had access to information that our organization couldn't hope to find. Tell me what you discovered about the Half Spur."

Helen was only too happy to oblige. The burden of what she suspected about her ex-husband's activities had been heavy for a long time. "Luckily, Franklin was so convinced of my stupidity that he was careless about safeguarding his secrets from me even after he knew I wanted a divorce. He left his laptop on the desk in his office without ever bothering to lock it away, and I soon found out that the password to his confidential files was *Superbowl.* I saw him type it in once, and after that I had free range of his computer."

"The guy should have stuck to playing football," Philip muttered. "He was pretty good at that."

"You were taking a huge risk in accessing Franklin's secret files," Ryan said grimly. "He's not only a powerful man. It's my belief he's a dangerous one."

There had been plenty of occasions when Helen had been terrified of what would happen if Franklin discovered her in his study. She hadn't been unaware of the risks she was running — just desperate.

She shrugged away the remembered fear. "I survived, thank goodness. That's the advantage of spying on your own husband — you know his habits and you can act accordingly. He always took his laptop with him when he left home, of course, but when he was home, I'd get up very early in the morning and spend an hour checking out various files. Franklin would still be sleeping long after I'd shut down the laptop and made myself breakfast. I was never tempted to push my luck and spend longer than an hour because I knew I could always come back the next day, or the one after that."

"It took Nell a while to figure out what she was actually seeing," Philip said. "She was fixated on the idea that the ranch was a tax haven, or a cover for illegal contributions, and none of the charts and graphs seemed to make financial sense."

"I was getting very frustrated," Helen agreed. "I quickly found out that Franklin had a silent partner in the Half Spur, but I never could fathom who it was."

"Do you know now?"

With regret, Helen shook her head. "Not for sure."

"But you have suspicions?"

"There was a man called Lio who used to hang out at the house a lot, and I suspect he's involved, but I can't prove it. I don't even know his full name. If Franklin's partner is this Lio person, he's hidden his ownership behind a facade of dummy corporations. I managed to unravel the trail back as far as an import-export company located in Nigeria, of all places. That was a complete dead end, though, so I was stymied in both aspects of my investigation. I couldn't confirm that Lio was Franklin's partner in the Half Spur, and the data I'd copied didn't tie in with my theory that the ranch was being used as a cover for illegal campaign contributions —"

"So I asked her to send me the files to see if I could come up with any insights that she was overlooking," Philip interjected. "But sending me the data was difficult —"

"I couldn't risk downloading the files onto a disk," Helen said. "Something I once overheard Franklin say suggested there might be a security protocol on his computer that would warn him if anyone tried to copy the Half Spur files."

"It was smart of you to be cautious," Ryan said, flashing her an approving glance. "So how did you get the data to your brother in the end?"

"I wrote it all down by hand." She gave a wry smile. "As you can imagine, that took a while. Fortunately, like I said before, time was one of the few things on my side. In the end, I just sat at Franklin's desk each morning and copied an hour's worth of data by hand, using regular old pen and paper. Then, when I had everything relevant, I mailed the data to Philip."

"And?" Ryan asked.

Helen smiled at her brother. "Since Philip didn't share my fixation with the idea that the ranch was designed as an operation that could launder illegal campaign contributions, he recognized at once that we were looking at medical records —"

"Not for people," Philip said. "But for the sheep Franklin keeps at the Half Spur. My eighteen months of med school didn't exactly equip me to be a brilliant medical detective, so I showed a sample of the data to one of my professors and asked him what we were looking at. He suggested it was research on some sort of self-replicating virus, possibly part of a test for an experimental vaccine. It seemed important information, but we had no idea what to do with it."

"Your professor's conclusion would tie in with everything my partners and I suspected." Ryan drew in a sharp breath. "My God! This could be really important, Nell. Precisely how long ago did you access these records?"

"More than a year ago. Between the end of June and the beginning of September last year, in fact. I'm sorry my data isn't more recent —"

"Don't apologize. The fact that your information dates from last year is what makes it so interesting." He looked at her intently. "Did you tell Franklin what you'd done, and what you suspected was going on at the Half Spur?"

Helen nodded. "That was how I got my divorce," she said simply.

Ryan drew in a shaky breath. "You're lucky Franklin didn't kill you. And I don't mean that as a joke."

"Don't worry, we had the precise same thoughts," Philip said.

"When I told him that I'd copied all his files about his operations at the Half Spur, I warned him that I'd made a statement about everything I knew, and that I'd sent the resulting documents to my lawyer and the Greek Orthodox priest from the parish where I grew up, along with copies of the data from Franklin's computer. And that the envelopes of information were currently sealed, but the lawyer and the priest had instructions that they were to be opened and delivered to both law enforcement and the media the moment the priest and the lawyer heard I was dead. It was a little hokey, I guess, but it worked."

Philip shot her a smile. "Here she is, you see. Alive and a free woman."

Ryan looked as if he wanted to make a comment to the effect that she was only alive and free until the moment Franklin found a way to wriggle out from the noose she'd constructed, but he restrained himself. Probably because he realized she was well aware of the fragility of her protection.

"And we don't believe the experiments at the Half Spur have stopped, of course," Philip turned toward Ryan. "We're guessing that's why Franklin keeps spreading rumors about Nell's mental health, and her supposed problems with alcohol. We figure Franklin is terrified she'll reveal what she knows, and so he's laying the groundwork to make sure that if either one of us goes public with our accusations, we're going to be dismissed as two more wackos with a crazy vendetta against a famous person."

Helen stood up, needing to stretch muscles that were cramped with tension. "Every time Franklin leaks some horrible new rumor about us we reconsider telling the media what we know," she said.

Philip ran his hand through his hair so that it stood up in spikes. "To be honest, I talked Helen out of going public on a couple of occasions. If we make accusations against Franklin and they don't stick, I'm afraid we'd be in real trouble. I honest to God think he's capable of ordering a hit on both of us out of sheer rage. And the documents Helen left with the priest and the lawyer wouldn't protect her anymore because they simply repeat the same information that already hadn't been sufficient to bring him down."

Ryan grimaced, his expression bleak. "I agree with you. Franklin Gettys is potentially capable of violence and you were probably smart to keep quiet about what you know. But that's where I come in. I'm sure my organization can help."

"How?" Helen asked bluntly.

"The only way you'll ever be truly safe is when Franklin Gettys is behind bars. We need to build a case against him, and I think the data you collected may provide the link we need to tie several threads from separate investigations together. There was an unusual outbreak of a disease with flulike symptoms in Silver Rapids early in the summer. It wasn't reported in the national press, so I doubt if you heard anything about it."

Helen and Philip shook their heads. "No, nothing," Philip said.

"Our clients and cases are confidential, so I can't provide details about how we did this, but our agency managed to identify viruses in the blood samples taken from sheep at the Half Spur and link them to the blood samples taken from the victims of the epidemic in Silver Rapids." He turned to Helen. "With his usual capacity for wriggling out of trouble, Franklin managed to convince the authorities that the similarities were coincidence. But now you have a completely separate set of data, dating from long before the epidemic, that might help us to establish a link he can't explain away."

Helen felt a spurt of relief that quickly dissipated. "But there's no way to prove I copied the information directly from Franklin's laptop, is there? And that means it's going to be my word against his, and you know who's going to sound more credible." She felt a surge of the sort of bitterness that had been absent from her life since the divorce. "There's never a way to pin anything on Franklin, dammit."

"Don't be so sure of that," Ryan said. "If you'll agree to send the data you collected to my partners back in Denver, I think we might be able to forge a real link between your ex-husband's sheep ranch and the epidemic in Silver Rapids." Helen could tell from his expression that he felt a growing excitement. "I have resources I can tap — people with extensive medical training — who'd do a great job of interpreting whatever information you can provide."

"You bet we agree," Helen exclaimed, exchanging a glance with her brother. "Philip and I are both sick to death of living in the shadow of Franklin's threats of vengeance."

Philip walked over to the phone and picked up a message pad and pencil, which he handed to Ryan. "Give me the address where you want the data sent. I transcribed all Helen's handwritten notes onto my computer months ago, so I can e-mail it right now to your office."

"This is great. I appreciate your willingness to help —"

Philip shook his head. "It's definitely my pleasure. I can't wait to see that scumbag nailed."

Ryan scribbled a few words and handed the page to Philip. "That's the e-mail address for Colleen Wellesley. Write a covering note telling her you've sent this information on my behalf and that it's extremely confidential, okay? I'll give her a call and explain what it is and how you acquired it."

"Okay, will do. See you in a bit." Philip headed for the stairs and his bedroom, his fast pace underscoring his eagerness to take some action against Franklin.

"Do you think there's a chance you can pool my information with yours and come up with enough evidence to get Franklin indicted?" Helen asked Ryan.

"That's the plan, but we have a way to go before we're at that point." He took out his cell phone. "But you've provided a valuable new angle for us to investigate, and our organization has the resources to keep digging until we discover exactly what's going on."

He gave her a surprisingly cheerful grin as he keyed in the numbers to reach Colleen Wellesley. "We'll nail the bastard, Nell. Count on it."

Ryan was still on the phone to Colleen Wellesley when Philip came back downstairs to report that the files had been e-mailed as promised. Leaving Ryan engrossed in his conversation, Helen and her brother carried the empty coffee mugs out to the kitchen.

"I have to get going," Philip said, setting the mugs in the sink. "I promised Cathie I'd be at her house hours ago. We've decided to leave early tomorrow morning for her parents' vacation cottage out on Anderson Island. We figure we should be safe from reporters there, not to mention the cops, the FBI and anybody else Franklin decides to send after us." He pointed to a scrap of paper stuck to the fridge door with a ladybug magnet. "That's the phone number if you need to be in touch."

"Thanks, although I doubt I'll need it."

"I'm hoping for a call saying that Franklin Gettys is in jail."

"You and me both." She sighed. "It's not

going to happen this weekend, though, so you and Cathie should relax and enjoy the break."

"We will. Neither of us has taken a vacation in months." Philip was halfway out the door when he turned back toward her, laughing.

"Share the joke," she said.

"It just struck me how annoyed Franklin would be if he realized that setting the media on my ass actually ended up helping you and Ryan get back together again."

Helen joined in his laughter. "Yes, you're right. There's definitely a twisted pleasure to be derived from that thought."

Philip sobered, giving her arm a light squeeze. "You know I'm only ducking out on you so that your slimy ex-husband can't use me to bring you any more grief."

"Yes, of course I realize that."

Philip shot her a speculative side glance. "And I want to give you and Ryan the chance to be alone for a day or two."

Helen was smart enough not to react to that unsubtle piece of brotherly prying. "Thank you," she said with admirable cool. "Ryan and I will enjoy catching up on old times." She gave Philip a quick hug before he could probe any more. "Tell Cathie I'll look forward to seeing her soon, okay?"

"Will do. Take care, Nell. I'm outta here." Philip touched his hand to his forehead in a mock salute. "I'm counting on you and Ryan to bring that creepy-crawly ex of yours to justice. Go get the bastard, and hang him out to dry."

Chapter Ten

Ryan had come to Seattle at the insistence of his colleagues in Colorado Confidential, the top-secret government agency that worked undercover behind the screen of the detective agency known as Investigations, Confidential and Undercover. He was as driven as his partners to find Sky Langworthy, but he had always thought this trip to Seattle was a wild-goose chase as far as Philip's involvement with the kidnapping was concerned. He'd only agreed to waste so much time because the trip provided a perfect excuse to see Helen again. It was way past time, he'd decided, to get Helen Kouros out of his system, once and for all. Unfortunately, instead of discovering she'd lost her power to enthrall him, he'd discovered that she was more desirable than ever.

When she'd stormed into the parlor, eyes flashing and hair flying, she'd looked nothing like the sleekly groomed society wife he'd seen at the Franklin Gettys's reception eighteen months earlier. Instead, he'd been confronted by a disheveled, sexy, luscious woman, with rain-dampened wisps of hair tumbling haphazardly onto her forehead. Her tousled hair and flashing eyes had reminded him all too vividly of the last morning he'd woken up with her in his bed. It had also reminded him — forcefully — that he wanted her back in his bed as soon as humanly possible.

The prospect of bringing down Franklin Gettys was one of the few things in the world currently capable of turning his thoughts from the splendor of Helen's legs and the length of time remaining before he could realistically expect to feel those legs wrapped around his naked body. Exerting maximum self-control, he focused one hundred percent of his attention on giving Colleen Wellesley a succinct account of everything Helen and Philip had told him, and answering his partner's volcanic eruption of questions.

Colleen was optimistic that the data Helen had copied from Franklin's computer would enlighten Colorado Confidential's experts as to exactly what experiments were being conducted on the sheep at the Half Spur, and she was hopeful they would be able to penetrate the barriers that screened Franklin's shadowy partners from discovery.

Even over the phone, Ryan could tell that Colleen was as excited as he was. His trip to Seattle was producing no immediately useful leads in the Langworthy case. But if baby Sky remained stubbornly lost, at least it seemed that there was finally a crack in the facade that Franklin Gettys presented to the world.

Ryan had just finished his call when Helen returned to the parlor carrying a tray of cheese and crackers, along with a bottle of wine and two glasses. "Philip has gone to his girlfriend's place for the weekend," she said, setting down the tray and reaching for a cracker. She added a cube of cheese and ate with evident pleasure. "Are you hungry? I'm starving. For some reason, rain always makes me hungry."

"Then you must be permanently in need of food," he said. "As far as I can see, it's always raining in this town."

She laughed, opening the wine with the efficiency of a former waitress. "No, the sun shines quite often. Truly."

"Sure. At least once a month. Maybe twice in August."

"Well, okay, the sky here tends to remain on the cloudy side. But rain's good for keeping the grass green. And the women here all have great complexions."

"Yeah. Especially if you like a bloom of mold on your cheeks."

She laughed again, a low, contented chuckle, and handed him a glass of wine. "This is from a local Washington vineyard. I was saving it for a special occasion, and I guess this is it." She lifted her glass in a toast, eyes sparkling. "To special occasions."

"And old friends reunited," he said, touching his glass to hers.

It had been a while since he had seen Helen looking so happy, Ryan reflected. In fact, the dazzling smile that had made her famous with regulars at the Swansong Casino had vanished almost as soon as she met Franklin Gettys. Until this moment, Ryan had believed that what he missed most about Helen was the incredible sex. Now he realized that, much as he yearned to make love to her again, of everything he missed about her, it was the absence of their shared laughter that had left the biggest gap in his life.

He was going to make damn sure that nothing ever happened to take the laughter away again, Ryan swore to himself. But he needed to move slowly, not rush her into making commitments that she wasn't ready for.

Helen returned to her previous seat on

the sofa, pulling the coffee table closer so that they could reach the platter of cheese. Ryan debated no more than a second or two before he sat down next to her. Hell, there was a difference between moving slowly and acting downright retarded.

He was close enough to smell her perfume, a subtle mix of fresh air and lavender shampoo. He crunched on a cracker, struggling to say something coherent other than *For God's sake, make love to me.*

Fortunately, Helen rescued him by inquiring about his sister. "Tell me what's happened with Becky's dancing career," she said. "I read that the show she was in closed after six months on Broadway. That was a pretty decent run."

"Enough to pay off her credit cards, which made her very happy. She was hoping it would last longer, of course, and make her world famous."

"Has she found another dancing job, or is she back to waiting tables?"

"She's just started touring with a new show," he said. "*Ipanema Express.* The out-of-town reviews have been great and the backers are planning to bring it to Broadway early next year, so Becky's ecstatic. One Broadway job might be considered sheer good luck, she says. Two mean she's a pro."

"That's fantastic news." Helen's face lit up. "If ever anyone deserved their professional success, it's your sister. Does the tour schedule include Seattle? I'd love to see her dance professionally."

"I'm not sure if they're coming here," he said. "But wait until the show makes it to New York next year and come see it with me."

She looked up at him, clearly startled by the invitation. "That would be lovely," she said, after a tiny pause. "I've never actually seen a live Broadway show."

"It's an experience you shouldn't miss. But be warned, it's addictive once you get started. You'll be planning trips to the Big Apple every year."

"Not unless I win the lottery." She pulled a face, but sounded perfectly cheerful, as if the lack of money didn't bother her much. "How about Becky's wedding plans?" she asked. "I know she and Jeff were talking about setting a date. Are they still engaged?"

"Who knows?" Ryan gave a wry grin. "They're still talking about getting married one day, but Jeff's dancing in Chicago right now, and Becky's in a different town every week. I don't know if they're ever going to reach the point where getting married is a priority for them. They're both pretty much obsessed with their careers."

Helen poured more wine into their glasses. "Then they're smart to postpone getting married, don't you think? It's probably not a good idea to get married chiefly because you both have a spare weekend in your schedules."

"I agree." He seized the chance to steer the conversation in a more personal direction. "What about you? Has your experience with Franklin turned you against the idea of marriage?"

Helen shook her head. "No. Almost the opposite, in fact. Going through the divorce helped me to see a lot of emotional stuff more clearly."

He aimed for casual and hoped he found it. "Care to share what you discovered?"

She was silent for a moment, searching for the right words. "When I agreed to marry Franklin I was way too hung up on what I thought I'd seen happening in my parents' marriage. I realize now I probably didn't see the truth. Kids usually don't. Besides, most of what I saw was my dad being a lousy parent, not a lousy husband. I guess I've wised up to the fact that Franklin and my dad are simply two messed-up individuals and I shouldn't make sweeping rules about men and relationships on the basis of their bad behavior."

Ryan was relieved that Helen's marriage hadn't left her with a general bias against men. He searched for a response that would prove he was a caring, sensitive, honorable person who should never be confused with a loser like her father, or a badass like Franklin Gettys. Unfortunately, his supply of warm and friendly social chitchat had apparently run dry. Bone-dry.

Maybe he should suggest taking her out to dinner, except that he had no desire to eat when it meant breaking the fragile bonds of intimacy growing again between the two of them. In truth, he wasn't in the mood either for food or conversation. Instead, his brain drummed out the message that right now they were alone in the house. Just the two of them. Alone.

His body absorbed the message.

Ryan reminded himself yet again that he needed to go slowly, that nothing good was likely to be achieved by rushing things. They needed time to explore the many and subtle changes that had occurred in the years since their separation. Maybe he should suggest dinner after all.

But he didn't make the suggestion. Instead, his head bent toward Helen, who was looking up at him, lips slightly parted and cheeks flushed. She was so incredibly beautiful, he thought, with skin like fresh blossoms on the magnolia trees in his grandmother's garden, creamy white with a heavenly tinge of pink. And where the hell did that poetic comparison come from? He was a man trained to think in terms of cold, hard fact, not flowers and metaphors.

His head dipped lower, and still lower. Then she was in his arms and his mouth was covering hers, and his body felt as if he'd stepped on a live electric wire.

Jesus, she tasted good! Her lips were soft and yielding and even more wonderful than he remembered. Her body molded against his, fitting within the circle of his arms as if they'd exchanged their last kiss only yesterday, instead of more than three years ago. He drowned in the taste of her, letting the scent of her soak into his skin. He felt as if a starved place deep inside him was slowly reviving after years of drought. How had he survived without her, he wondered. How in hell had he done it?

When she left him for Franklin Gettys, Ryan had been so furious that she could do something so crazy — so totally insane — that pure rage had carried him through the first few weeks of their separation. Eventually, though, his anger had died away, and he was left with a painful awareness of how bitterly he missed her.

He resigned as sheriff of Silver Rapids, moved to Denver, signed on as a cop, and dated other women. Lots of other women, although what he was trying to prove he hadn't been quite sure. Now he knew. He'd always recognized that the hurt of separating from Helen had been severe, but even he hadn't realized how deeply the hurt had gone. He'd grown so accustomed to the ache of her loss that it had become part of the furniture of his life, something that couldn't be moved and so had to be accommodated. He'd tried to smother his pain in a cushion of other women.

Now, with Helen in his arms once again, with her mouth open beneath his, her legs twined around him, and her breasts pressed against his chest, he could see just how devastatingly hollow the years without her had been. When she'd left him, Ryan had sworn he'd never allow himself to be vulnerable to a woman again.

It was a good vow, he thought wryly. Pity that with Helen back in his life, he didn't have a hope in hell of sticking to it.

They broke apart, mostly because he needed to draw breath. But it was also a pathetic attempt to prove to himself that he was still enough in control of his emotions to do it. Helen looked up at him, and the light from the floor lamp by the hearth made her eyes appear almost golden. She was the one who spoke first.

"I used to think making love came too easily for us," she said, her voice husky. "We never had to work at our relationship. It was just — there, right from the start."

"Most people would consider that a miracle."

"But not me." Her voice filled with self-mockery. "Smart woman that I was, I figured that what we shared couldn't be worth much or it would demand more effort from us." She shook her head in bafflement. "How could I have been so . . . ignorant? I wasn't sixteen. I was twenty-seven and old enough to know better. I can't believe I threw away something so incredibly valuable."

Ryan took her hand and pressed a kiss into her palm, about all he could trust himself to do at this precise moment. "Is that why you married Franklin Gettys? Because loving me was too easy?"

She flushed, embarrassed. "That sounds crazy."

"Yeah, I'd have to say pretty much."

She smiled, but there were shadows around the smile. "It *was* crazy, as I soon found out. I married Franklin because I thought he represented stability and security and everything that was practical and rational about choosing a lifetime partner. What I learned . . ." Her voice died away.

He took her face and framed it in his hands. "What did you learn?" From the darkness in her eyes it was obvious that the lesson had been hard won.

"I guess I learned that security in a marriage comes from loving and trusting your partner, not from marrying someone who has a respected position or a large income. But even more important, I learned that if you're ever lucky enough to find romance and passion and happiness and laughter in the company of another human being, you should grab on to the relationship with both hands and never let go."

That sounded promising, Ryan thought. "When you talk about grabbing a happy relationship and hanging on tight, are you talking in general terms here, Nell, or are you being specific?"

"I'm being specific. Sort of, anyway." She drew in a shaky breath. "I realize you may have moved on, Ryan. I mean, why wouldn't you? I know there must be a zillion women out there that you could date. And . . . and marry, if that's what you want to do. You're an incredibly sexy man —"

He was certainly pleased to hear that she thought so. He pressed his forefinger against her lips, his emotions nearly as tumultuous as her words. "Nell, honey, I'm having trouble translating. What exactly are you trying to say?"

For answer, she bit the pad of his finger and linked her hands behind his neck, pulling his head down to hers. "I'm trying to say . . . I missed you, Ryan. I missed you a lot. Kiss me again. Or better yet, take me to bed and make love to me for the rest of the night."

He spoke against her mouth, his hands already working on the buttons of her blouse. "Honey, I can't remember the last time I was so delighted to oblige a lady."

"Woman . . ." she murmured, as he pushed her shirt off her shoulders. "I'm a woman, not a lady."

"That's good news, because I'm sure as hell not feeling much like a gentleman." Ryan bent to nuzzle her breasts, his hand searching under the hem of her skirt and moving upward.

"Oh my God," she murmured.

"Yeah," he said. "My thoughts exactly."

Her hand reached for the buckle of his belt and then for the zipper of his jeans. He groaned, but held her gaze. “Oh my God.”

“Yeah,” she whispered, laughter in her eyes. “My thoughts exactly.”

It was the last thing either of them said for a very long time.

Chapter Eleven

Helen stirred lazily in the bed, swimming up toward consciousness through a warm, tropical sea of sensation. Gradually her drowsiness dissolved into full awareness of her surroundings: Ryan's hand resting on her hip, the repletion of her body, the soothing splatter of raindrops against the window panes. She nestled closer to Ryan and found the perfect place for her head on the crook of his outspread arm.

"It's raining again," she mumbled, still half asleep.

He traced a lazy pattern over her neck and shoulders. "What a surprise."

She gave a soft laugh. "It makes a great excuse not to get out of bed."

"I can think of better ones." He leaned over and kissed the hollow of her neck in the precise spot that was guaranteed to drive her wild. Her breath caught and her skin flushed with instant heat, although a few hours ago she had been so sated from their lovemaking that she'd assumed it would be days before she felt real desire again.

"Do you miss the Colorado sunshine?" Ryan asked, his thumb stroking tantalizingly across her nipple.

"Sometimes, especially the clear skies and the brilliant colors." She stirred beneath his touch, trying to hold on to the thread of their conversation when her body was already trembling with anticipation. "Seattle's a wonderful city and I love being close to the ocean, but I guess I'm a Coloradan at heart."

"Come back to Denver with me," he said, his hands suddenly still.

Her heart skipped a beat. "For the weekend?"

"Forever." He raised himself on one elbow and looked down at her and the intensity of emotion she saw in his eyes made her heart skip a beat.

"I love you," Ryan said. "And I'm pretty sure you love me."

Her smile deepened. "I think I may have mentioned something about that a couple of times last night."

His hand trailed lower to draw the shape of a heart on her stomach. "It doesn't count when you're begging for sex. Say it again now, when you aren't desperate to have me inside you."

"I love you," Helen said, her voice husky. She looked up at him, laughing. "Especially when I'm begging for sex."

He kissed her on the tip of her nose, but his gaze remained serious. "We've already wasted almost four years of our lives living apart," he said. "I can't think of a single reason to waste any more time. Can you?"

She raised her hand and cradled it against Ryan's cheek. "Not a one." They'd both grown and changed, Helen reflected, but that didn't mean they'd changed in ways that had driven them apart. She realized now that the passion she and Ryan shared was a rare gift, almost as rare as the comfortable intimacy they were already beginning to recapture. She'd thrown that gift away once before but she wasn't going to make the same mistake twice.

They made love again, with a slow sweetness that built to a climax of shattering power. She was still drifting back down to earth when Ryan sat up and moved around the bed until he was kneeling in front of her, the sheets rumpled across his knees.

"Marry me, Nell."

The last time he'd proposed to her they'd been in Silver Rapids's fanciest restaurant, dressed in formal clothes, and he'd been holding a blue velvet jewelry box open to display a diamond solitaire engagement ring. Helen liked the setting for this proposal much better.

She sat up and knelt facing him, laughing as she threw her arms around his neck, kissing him hard and long. "Yes, yes, Ryan. Of course I'll marry you."

Ryan remained rigidly unmoving for about ten seconds. Then the reality of her acceptance sank in and he dragged her off the bed, sweeping her into his arms and waltzing around the tiny bedroom.

The ring of his cell phone on the nightstand beside the bed interrupted their impromptu dance. "Damn!" he said. "I have to get that. Only people at work have the number." He flipped open his phone. "Yes, this is Ryan."

He listened intently, then turned to give Helen the thumbs-up sign. "They've already started working on your data," he said, covering the mouthpiece. "They're ecstatic about how much information you've given them."

"I'm glad it's useful."

"I'll be back in the office on Monday," he said into the phone, taking his hand away from the mouthpiece. He paused to listen.

"No, I can't come back today. I'll fly out of here either Sunday night or Monday morning."

Helen couldn't hear what the caller was saying, but he or she obviously asked what was keeping Ryan in Seattle.

Ryan's eyes lit up with silent amusement as he replied. "I'm making arrangements to get married," he said and shut the phone, tossing it onto the bed.

"That was Colleen Wellesley," he informed Helen.

The phone rang again before he could say anything more, sending him rummaging through the bedcovers to find it.

"Yes?" he said, flicking it open.

Even from the other side of the bed, Helen could hear the torrent of words gushing from the caller.

"Colleen, stop asking questions long enough for me to reply." Ryan kept a straight face, but his voice hovered on the edge of open laughter. "First answer:

"Helen Kouros. Second answer: As soon as she'll set the date. Third answer: We're dancing naked around the bedroom. Fourth answer: No, because I'm not answering the phone any more today. I'll check in again tomorrow morning. Fifth answer: Goodbye."

He shut the phone and put it on the

nightstand. "Be grateful that Seattle is a thousand miles away from Denver," he said. "Otherwise Colleen would already be in her car by now, en route to visit us. Probably trailing half the office staff behind her."

Helen smiled, slipping on her robe. "I wouldn't mind. I'm looking forward to meeting your partners."

"They're interesting people," Ryan acknowledged, pulling on his jeans and the sweater he'd worn the day before.

"What did Colleen originally call about, before she got sidetracked into being amazed by the news that you're getting married?" Helen asked as they made their way downstairs in pursuit of breakfast.

"She wanted to let me know that she considers the information you've provided, combined with everything we already know, the beginning of the end for Franklin Gettys," Ryan said with quiet conviction. "Bribing cops and corrupting the justice system is only the tip of the iceberg as far as his criminal activities are concerned, I'm sure of it. It may take us a while longer before he's behind bars, but we're going to bring him down."

She wanted Franklin brought to justice, but Helen was astonished at how irrelevant his activities seemed to her now, despite his fifteen months of constant harassment. Why would she choose to stay mired in the past, a captive to Franklin's vindictive schemes, when she could walk into the future with Ryan?

She stared at him as he poured water into the coffeemaker, overcome by a sudden rush of emotion. "What is it?" he asked, searching her face. "What's wrong?"

"Nothing," she said. She laughed, her breath catching, and moved into his arms. "I just realized that I really, really love you."

He framed her face with his hands. "What took you so long?"

"Just a slow learner, I guess."

"Good thing I'm a patient man." His kiss was tender and rich with promise.

"Look," she said, her head on his shoulder. "The sun's come out. It's going to be a fine day, after all."

"It sure is," Ryan said. "A very fine day."

Epilogue

The offices of Colorado Confidential at the Royal Flush Ranch, Four days later

Her security monitor beeped, warning Colleen Wellesley that a car had just crossed the electronic perimeter fence and turned into the Royal Flush driveway. She recognized Ryan's dark blue Pathfinder, and quelled a sudden flare of nervousness. This was going to be her first meeting with Helen Kouros, and for Ryan's sake, she wanted it to go well.

She opened the file containing a printout of the material that had been e-mailed to her by Helen's brother on Friday night. She leafed through the forty pages of closely packed data, astonished all over again that Helen had managed to acquire so much confidential information without Franklin's knowledge. Colleen could only imagine the difficulty of writing out so many columns of figures by hand, with painstaking accuracy, and she admired Helen's persistence, not to mention her skill in avoiding detection.

The material from Franklin's laptop had turned out to be a treasure trove of vital insights into the illegal experiments being conducted at the Half Spur. Combined with information already in the possession of Colorado Confidential, Colleen was hopeful that a compelling criminal case could be built against Franklin Gettys. After two years of trying, it seemed they were finally getting the facts to back up their suspicions.

Despite her gratitude to Helen, Colleen still harbored some doubts as to whether a woman who had been married to Senator Franklin Gettys could ever make a suitable wife for Ryan Benton. She discounted the rumors she'd heard about Helen's drinking problems and her numerous affairs because she knew those rumors had been circulated by Franklin Gettys and that automatically made them suspect. Still, she'd seen Helen at a couple of fund-raisers when she was still married to the senator, and Colleen hadn't been favorably impressed. Helen was certainly beautiful, with lovely facial features and a dancer's lithe and supple body, but Colleen hadn't detected a trace of warmth or spontaneity in her. You would expect a man as smart and insightful as Ryan Benton to realize that it would be no fun to marry an ice princess, but Colleen had learned from experience that men had a hard time paying attention to a woman's character flaws when they came wrapped in a package as enticing as Helen's.

The security system delivered another warning. Ryan was escorting Helen through the outer offices of the Royal Flush ranch and approaching the secret meeting room where Colleen waited to greet them. Her gaze fixed on the monitor, Colleen studied Helen while Ryan keyed in the code that would cause the wine rack to swing inward and give him access to the offices of Colorado Confidential.

Until now, Colleen had never seen Helen dressed in anything except expensive evening gowns, but today she was wearing jeans and a lemon-yellow cotton sweater and she still managed to look fabulous. On her, the everyday outfit looked like a high-fashion statement. The monitor was clear enough to show that she was wearing almost no makeup, and her hair was pulled back from her face in a loose and rumpled chignon. On most women, that sort of hairstyle looked a mess. On Helen, the wisps and haphazard strands looked like a style favored by movie stars who didn't want to appear as if they'd just spent five hours with their hairdresser.

The woman was seriously sexy, Colleen decided. More than attractive enough to screw with Ryan's mind.

Ryan came into the meeting room, his arm around Helen, his eyes glowing. "Okay, Colleen, here she is, fresh off the plane from Seattle." His voice was full of pride, his body language replete with love. "This is my fiancée, Helen Kouros. Honey, this is my boss, Colleen Wellesley."

Helen smiled, not the professional smile Colleen had seen at the senator's fund-raisers, but a warm smile, tinged with just a hint of shyness. "It's such a pleasure to meet you," Helen said, holding out her hand. "While we were driving out from the airport, Ryan told me more about the case you're trying to build against Franklin Gettys. I'm hoping so much that the information I copied from his laptop has provided you with some useful leads. Has it?"

Colleen was hard put to believe that this soft-spoken woman was the same person she'd seen standing stiff and unapproachable at Franklin Gettys's side. Belatedly, it occurred to her that in view of everything Colorado Confidential now knew about the senator's criminal activities, it was no wonder that Helen had always seemed so cool and withdrawn. Living as the wife of

Franklin Gettys would be enough to drive any sensitive, openhearted woman into a state where total repression of her true feelings was the only way to retain her sanity. Her attitude toward Helen thawed the final few degrees.

"The information you provided has been invaluable," Colleen said. "But first things first. It's great to have you here, Helen. May I get you something to drink? Or something to eat? I know they never feed people on flights nowadays."

"Nothing for me, thanks," Helen said, shaking her head.

"How about you, Ryan?"

"Thanks, but we're going out to dinner as soon as we leave here," Ryan said, pulling up a chair for Helen, and looking as if it required all his willpower not to lean over and kiss her.

"We're going house-hunting after we've eaten," Helen explained. She dragged her gaze away from Ryan, her cheeks suddenly flaring with heat.

Good grief, Colleen thought in silent amusement. *They're about ready to tear each other's clothes off.*

"Then I'll try to keep this as brief as possible," she said, pretending not to notice the sudden increase in sexual tension that flooded the room. She turned to look directly at Helen. "The charts and statistics you copied from the senator's computer were more valuable than we could possibly have hoped or imagined. They filled in some vital blanks in other information that we'd recovered from various sources, and the bottom line is that — based on the package of information we've been able to provide — the local FBI office is launching an official investigation of Franklin Gettys —"

"That is truly good news." Helen's body slumped with relief. "Is my brother right about what Franklin was doing? Was he using the sheep as part of some sort of unauthorized medical experiment?"

"In a way," Colleen said. "Although we believe he was involved in something much more threatening than that. We believe the sheep at the Half Spur are part of an experiment involving biological weapons."

"My God!" Helen gulped. "Biological weapons?"

"That's what we think," Colleen acknowledged.

Helen appeared unable to grasp the enormity of it. "I know Franklin is always preaching that the only way to protect ourselves from maniacs like Saddam Hussein is to have the same sort of weapons capability that he did, but I still can't believe Franklin would take the law into his own hands like that."

"Believe it," Ryan said, his voice grim. "Remember the flu epidemic in Silver Rapids that I mentioned to you?"

Helen nodded.

"Well, we think that Franklin, either accidentally or purposely, ran a test that ended up infecting the people of the town."

Helen was quiet for a few seconds, and the happy light in her eyes died away. "I was married to a monster," she said finally. "How could I not have known that he was such a terrible person? How could I have stayed married to him for three weeks, let alone nearly three years? Why didn't I sense the darkness in him right from the start?"

Ryan took her hand and held it cradled in his. "Don't blame yourself," he said. "Put the blame where it belongs, which is squarely with Franklin Gettys. Here's a man who had everything — a great career as a college athlete and then as a professional footballer, followed by the honor of winning election to the United States senate. Most people would have been overwhelmed with gratitude for their good fortune, but not Franklin. Instead of striving to serve the people of Colorado to the best of his ability, he turns around and uses his office as a power base to pursue his insane vision of bio weapons that can be unleashed on the unsuspecting world."

"You have nothing to blame yourself for," Colleen said, adding her own reassurance to Ryan's. "Remember, without the information you copied from Franklin's laptop, there would be no FBI investigation and virtually no chance that the senator might soon be indicted."

"At least that's some consolation," Helen said. "I guess."

"And there's more," Ryan said. "About the kidnapping of Sky Langworthy —"

"Oh, have you found him? That would be truly wonderful." Helen's expressive face shone with hope, and Colleen wondered how she could ever have imagined that this woman was aloof and unemotional.

"We haven't found Sky yet." Colleen permitted herself the luxury of a sigh. Their continued failure to locate Holly Langworthy's baby ate at her soul, day and night. "As you know, the data you copied from the senator's laptop predates Sky's disappearance by several months. But there is some very interesting e-mail correspondence between your ex-husband and a man called Lio —"

Helen nodded. "Yes, I copied that because I'm sure Lio is at least part owner of the Half Spur with Franklin. Unfortunately, I have no idea who Lio is, or what he does, or where he lives —"

"We might be able to fill in some of the blanks for you," Colleen said. "We believe that Lio may in fact be Helio DeMarco —"

"Helio DeMarco?" Helen queried.

"The organized crime boss," Ryan explained. "We knew DeMarco was operating in Colorado, and we suspected there might be some involvement with Sky's disappearance, but your computer notes give us a totally new lead to explore. Thanks to you, we're more hopeful of a break in the Langworthy case right now than we have been in several weeks."

"All in all, we're in your debt," Colleen said, smiling. "Thank you, Helen."

"No, it's the other way around," Helen said, rising to her feet. "I'm deeply in *your* debt. The knowledge that I might have contributed something useful to solving the Langworthy kidnapping and getting Franklin Gettys put behind bars makes me feel a lot less angry about those final months of my marriage. Perhaps they weren't the terrible waste I've always assumed."

"And on that positive note, we're out of

here." Ryan put his arm back around Helen's waist, and she melted against him. He looked down at her, his gaze tender, then turned back to Colleen. "Okay, we're off in search of dinner and a new home."

"We've decided we'll get married as soon as we find the right house," Helen added.

They looked so happy together that it made Colleen feel wistful. "Good luck with your house-hunting," she said.

Ryan and Helen left the meeting room and the secret door slid back into place. Picking up the latest field reports, Colleen redirected her attention to the demanding task of finding Sky Langworthy. Whatever it took, she was going to give Holly back her baby and bring his kidnappers to justice. That was a promise.

About the Author

Jasmine Cresswell is a multitalented author of over forty novels. Her efforts have gained her numerous awards, including the RWA's Golden Rose Award and the Colorado Author's League Award for the best original paperback novel. Born in Wales and educated in England, Jasmine met her husband while working at the British Embassy in Rio de Janeiro. She has lived in Australia, Canada and six cities in the United States. Jasmine and her husband now make their home in Sarasota, Florida.

We hope you have enjoyed this Large Print book. Other Thorndike, Wheeler or Chivers Press Large Print books are available at your library or directly from the publishers.

For more information about current and upcoming titles, please call or write, without obligation, to:

Publisher
Thorndike Press
295 Kennedy Memorial Drive
Waterville, ME 04901
Tel. (800) 223-1244

Or visit our Web site at:
www.gale.com/thorndike
www.gale.com/wheeler

OR

Chivers Large Print
published by BBC Audiobooks Ltd
St James House, The Square
Lower Bristol Road
Bath BA2 3SB
England
Tel. +44(0) 800 136919
email: bbcaudiobooks@bbc.co.uk
www.bbcaudiobooks.co.uk

All our Large Print titles are designed for easy reading, and all our books are made to last.